Hannah was about to go in search of Leonidas when he strode into the room, wearing only a pair of swimming shorts and a look that—in the seconds before surprise contorted his expression—showed his impatience with her arrival.

He was partying.

He was probably the center of attention, being just as fawned over and celebrated as his brother. Jealousy tore through her, but Hannah told herself it was outrage. Outrage that she'd been agonizing over their baby while he'd slipped out of bed and gone back to his normal life as though it had never happened.

If she'd held even a single shred of hope that he might be glad to see her, it disappeared immediately.

"Hannah." His eyes roamed her face and then dropped lower, until he was staring at her stomach and she felt the force of his shock, the reverberation of his confusion. It slammed into the room, slammed against her, and if she weren't so consumed with her own feelings, she might almost have felt sympathy for him.

"Yes," she answered the unspoken question, her voice slightly shaky. "I'm pregnant. And you're the father."

Clare Connelly

THE GREEK'S BILLION-DOLLAR BABY

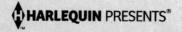

Recycling programs
for this product may
not exist in your area.

ISBN-13: 978-1-335-53869-7

The Greek's Billion-Dollar Baby

First North American publication 2019

Copyright © 2019 by Clare Connelly

This edition published by arrangement with Harlequin Books S.A.

For questions and comments about the quality of this book, please contact us at CustomerService@Harlequin.com.

Printed in U.S.A.

For Emma Darcy, who wrote the first Harlequin
I ever read and thus gave me one of the greatest
gifts of my life—an enduring love of passionate,
escapist romance.

There is a piece of Emma Darcy in every book
I write.

Clare Connelly was raised in small-town Australia among a family of avid readers. She spent much of her childhood up a tree, Harlequin romance book in hand. Clare is married to her own real-life hero and they live in a bungalow near the sea with their two children. She is frequently found staring into space—a surefire sign she is in the world of her characters. She has a penchant for French food and ice-cold champagne, and Harlequin novels continue to be her favorite-ever books. Writing for Harlequin Presents is a long-held dream. Clare can be contacted via clareconnelly.com or on her Facebook page.

Books by Clare Connelly

Harlequin Presents

Innocent in the Billionaire's Bed
Bought for the Billionaire's Revenge
Her Wedding Night Surrender
Bound by the Billionaire's Vows
Spaniard's Baby of Revenge

Secret Heirs of Billionaires

Shock Heir for the King

Christmas Seductions

Bound by Their Christmas Baby
The Season to Sin

Harlequin DARE

Guilty as Sin

Her Guilty Secret
His Innocent Seduction

Visit the Author Profile page
at Harlequin.com for more titles.

PROLOGUE

BEING EQUAL NUMBER TWO on the international rich list might have made Leonidas Stathakis the envy of the world, but Leonidas knew from personal experience that money was a poor substitute for having what you really wanted in life.

Billions in the bank didn't take away the empty throb of loss that dogged your steps when you'd had to bury your loved ones.

Being rich didn't take away the grief, nor the guilt, nor the pain and the sense of impotence at knowing you had put someone in harm's way—that you had failed to protect them.

This was his fourth New Year's Eve without his family. The fourth year he'd seen draw to a close with only memories of his wife, Amy, and their two-year-old son, Brax.

It felt like a lifetime.

When he closed his eyes, he saw her as clearly as if she were standing in front of him. He'd never forget the way she smiled, as though she'd struck a match inside and happiness was exploding out of her.

How could someone so full of life and vitality simply cease to exist? For all her strength, she'd been so weak at the end, so fragile. Ploughed into while walking Brax to the playground. What chance did either of their bodies stand against that hunk of metal, commanded by a madman?

Hair that had been a vibrant russet with eyes that were the same shade as the ocean beyond this hotel; he saw her as she'd been in life, and then, as she'd been in death.

He would never forget Amy Stathakis, nor the violent fate that had awaited her, murdered because of his father's criminal activities.

Dion Stathakis had destroyed their family, and, with Amy and Brax's death, had destroyed Leonidas's life.

Anger surged inside him and he curved his fingers more tightly about his Scotch glass, wondering how many of these he'd had. Not so many as to dull the pain yet, though in his experience it took more than a few quick drinks in a bar to get anywhere near the obliteration he sought. Especially at times like this, when his memories were at their clearest.

Happiness surrounded him. Loud, exuberant noises of celebration. People seemed to love marking the close of a year, celebrating the arrival of a new one, and he could understand that. At one time, he'd felt just the same—he had celebrated life with Amy.

Now, every day was something to be got

through. Every year was simply something he survived—without them. His very existence was a betrayal. How many times had he thought he would give his life to return theirs? He was the son of the criminal bastard—he, Leonidas, should have paid for his father's crimes. Not his innocent wife and their beautiful son.

Bitterness threatened to scorch him alive.

He threw his Scotch back and, without his signalling for another, a hostess arrived at his table, replacing it with a substitute, just as he'd requested. There were some perks to being the owner of the place, and this was one of them.

He lifted his head towards her in acknowledgement, noting dispassionately how attractive she was. Blonde hair, brown eyes, a caramel tan and pale pink lips that were quick to turn into a smile. A nice figure, too. She had the kind of looks he had once found irresistible.

But not any more.

Yes, he could have opened himself to the hint of desire that stirred inside him. That started in his gut and, as his eyes dropped to her breasts, to the hint of lace he could see beneath the cotton shirt she wore, spread like flame, threatening to make him hard right there in the skyline view bar of his six-star hotel on Chrysá Vráchia.

But he refused the impulse. He turned his attention to his Scotch, taking pleasure in denying his body any hint of satisfaction on that score. It had been four years. Four years without Amy, four years without knowing the pleasure of a woman. It was a habit he had no intention of breaking…

CHAPTER ONE

HANNAH HADN'T COME to Chrysá Vráchia to lose her virginity.

She hadn't come to this stunning Greek island for any reason other than she'd been in shock and needed to escape Australia. Her controlling aunt, uncle, and the cousin she'd thought of as a sister—who'd been sleeping with Hannah's fiancé.

She'd discovered them in bed together and been at the airport two hours later, booking the first available flight—which just happened to bring her here.

This stunning paradise she'd heard of all her life and wanted to visit. Golden cliffs, white sand beaches, turquoise waters, lush green forests— it was paradise on earth and the perfect place to chew through her honeymoon savings and re-build her heart.

So apparently even the darkest storm clouds had silver linings.

No, Hannah hadn't come to Greece to lose her virginity but as her eyes kept straying to the man across the hotel bar, she felt the pull of desire deep in her chest, and something more.

Vengeance? Anger? No. It was less barbaric than that, less calculated.

Fascination.

She looked at the man across from her, cradling his Scotch with a brooding intensity that tied her tummy in knots, and she felt a surge of white-hot desire that was as unfamiliar as it was intriguing.

Waiting until they were married had been Angus's idea, but she'd gone along with it. She loved Angus, she liked the way he made her feel, the way he kissed her and held her tight. But she'd never really longed for him. She'd never trembled at his touch nor fallen asleep imagining his kisses.

And the idea of carelessly giving something away to a stranger, sleeping with a man she didn't know, felt like the perfect way to respond to her fiancé cheating on her with her cousin.

Hannah's chest tightened as flashbacks of that moment sliced through her. It was too raw. Too fresh.

Still…he looked like a man who wanted to be left alone. As she watched, a blonde waitress approached and said something *sotto voce*. He didn't even meet her eyes when he responded, instead looking towards the view beyond them, the dark night sky inky for now—though it would soon be illuminated with the fireworks that marked the conclusion of one year and the start of another.

Midnight ticked closer and Hannah sipped her champagne thoughtfully.

She'd never approached a man before. She had no idea what to say. And it was a stupid idea. Hannah was twenty-three years old; there was a reason she was so woefully inexperienced with the opposite sex.

She was completely clueless.

No way could she click her fingers and change her personality, even if she wanted to.

Suppressing a sigh, she stood and moved towards the bar. If she wasn't going to do something *really* out of character and have a random one-night stand with a stranger, then she could do something *slightly* out of character and get a little bit tipsy.

She stood and looked about for a waiter, moving to the other side of her table, and deciding to go direct to the bar when she couldn't find one. But as she spun to the bar she connected with something impossibly hard and broad.

Something strong and firm, like concrete. Something that almost sent her flying across the room for the latent strength contained within its frame.

A hand snaked out to steady her and Hannah lifted her gaze, right into the obsidian eyes of the man she'd been unable to look away from for the past hour. He was rubbing his shoulder distractedly and a little pain radiated from her own, so she presumed they'd bumped into each other—hard.

'It's you,' she exhaled on a tremulous breath, trying to swallow even when her mouth was bone dry.

'It's me,' he agreed, his expression unchanging.

'You're like a brick wall,' she said before she could stop herself. The man's brows furrowed, and, if anything, he looked even hotter when he was all handsome and forbidding.

'Are you hurt?'

My pride is hurt. My heart is hurt. But this was not what he was asking. 'No, I'm fine.' And something like courage lashed at her spine, so she heard herself say, 'But I should at least buy you a drink. For getting in your way.'

A stern expression crossed his face and she felt the beginnings of embarrassment, certain he was going to say 'no', that she'd just made a complete fool of herself.

She bit down on her lower lip, wishing she could recall the words to her mouth. He stared at her for a long time, saying nothing, and with every second that passed her heart rate accelerated; she was drowning.

'That is not necessary,' he said, but made no effort to move. That alone was buoying. At least, Hannah hoped it was.

Her fingertips shook a little as she lifted them to her hair, straightening the auburn mane behind her ear. His eyes followed the gesture, a contemplative frown on his face.

'I wasn't watching where I was going,' she said.

'Nor was I. In which case, I should buy you a drink.'

Hannah's heart turned over in her chest, desire like a wave that had picked her up and was dragging her with it.

'How about I buy this round and you can get the next?' she said with a lift of one brow.

It was by the far the most forward she'd ever been in her life but seeing Angus in bed with Michelle had robbed Hannah of the ability to feel embarrassment.

His frown deepened. Then, he nodded a little, just a shift of his head. 'You have a deal, Miss…'

'Hannah,' she said, her own name emerging a little husky. She darted her tongue out and licked the outline of her lower lip, her eyes holding his so she saw the way the black shifted, morphing to inky and coal.

'Hannah,' he repeated, his European accent

doing funny things to the simple two syllables, so her gut lurched.

'And you are?'

Surprise briefly flashed on his features. 'Leonidas.'

His name was just what she'd expect. Masculine, spicy and sexy, it suited him to a T.

'You have a table?' she asked, shifting her eyes to where he was sitting. A couple had already claimed it. She spun around and saw the same fate had befallen her own seat.

'I was just on my way to my room.' He said the words slowly, the frown not leaving his face, the statement almost spoken against his will.

But the question in the words didn't fail to reach Hannah's ears, nor her awakening libido. Desire throbbed low down in her abdomen, so heat flamed through her.

'Were you?'

Plan for seduction or not, Hannah knew she was moving dramatically out of her realm of experience.

'It has a view back towards Athens. Perhaps we could have our drink on my balcony?'

Hannah had no idea if he was seriously offering to show her the view, or if this invitation was for so much more—she hoped the latter, and had every intention of finding out.

It was stupid. So stupid, so completely out of

character, but she wasn't acting from a rational place. Hannah had had her heart and trust broken and, wounded, she needed something. She needed to know she was desirable. She wanted to know what sex was all about. She had to push Angus way out of her mind.

And this man with his darkly quizzical gaze and mysterious, brooding face was everything she wanted—for one night only.

'I…' This was it. Her moment of truth. Could she do this?

The bar was busy and a woman passed behind Hannah, knocking her forward so Hannah's body was once again pushed against Leonidas's. This time, his hand reached out to steady her but it lingered, curving around her back and holding her there. Her eyes lifted to his, and doubts filled her. They were mirrored back to her, a look of confusion in his eyes, uncertainty on his face.

'I want you to come upstairs with me.' He said the words almost as though they were a revelation, as though he was completely surprised by the pull of this desire.

Hannah's pulse was like a torrent of lava, hot and demanding in her bloodstream. She wanted that too, more than anything.

'I just got out of a relationship,' she heard herself saying, her expression unknowingly shifting so her green eyes were laced with sadness.

'I was engaged, actually, until recently. I'm not looking for anything. You know, anything more than…' She looked away, shyness unwelcome, yet impossible to disguise.

'I don't do relationships,' the man said quietly. 'I don't generally do one-night stands, either.'

Generally.

The word was like an axe, preparing to fall. Hannah's eyes slid back to his and the hand that was at her back, holding her pressed to him, began to move up a little, running over her spine with a possessive inquiry that warmed her from the inside out.

'Nor do I.'

'Theos…' He said the word under his breath. 'I didn't come here for this.'

There was an undercurrent of emotion to his words, a sense of powerlessness that pulled at Hannah's heartstrings. And if she weren't completely drowning in this torrent of desire, she might have asked him about it. She might have insisted they find somewhere to talk. But desire was taking over Hannah's body, and she reached her hand around behind her back so her fingers could lace with his.

'Nor did I.'

His eyes glittered as they saw right through her, boring into her soul. 'A night out of time,' he said, pulling her with him, away from the bar, weaving with skill and ease towards the glass doors that led to the hotel foyer.

People seemed to move for him—he had a silent strength that conveyed itself with every step he took.

And with every inch they covered, Hannah's mind was yelling at her that this was stupid, that she was going to regret this, even as her heart and sex drive were applauding her impetuosity.

The hotel had been more than Hannah had expected, despite its billing as one of the world's finest. It was true six-star luxury, from the white marble floor to the gold columns that extended to the triple-height ceilings, the glossy grand piano in one corner being expertly played by a renowned pianist, the enormous crystal chandeliers that hung overhead.

As they approached the lifts, a suited bellhop dipped his head in deferential welcome. 'Good evening, sir,' he murmured. 'Madam.'

His gloved hand pressed the button to call the lift and Hannah stood beside Leonidas, waiting in complete silence. The lift arrived seconds later and Leonidas stood back, allowing Hannah to enter before him.

She stepped into the plush interior, her breath held, her senses rioting with the madness of what she was about to do.

But the moment she felt regret or doubt, she

closed her eyes and conjured the image of Angus's pale face brightened by his sensual exertions with Michelle and determination kicked inside her.

Not that she needed it—desire alone was propelling her through this, but anger was a good backup.

'You are no longer engaged?'

The lift pulled upwards, but that wasn't why her stomach swooped.

'No,' she said. 'I've left him—everyone—far behind.'

'You are angry?'

'No.' She was. And she wasn't. She was... hurt. Reeling. Confused. And if she *was* angry, it was mostly with herself, for having been so stupid as to believe him, to care for him, to get so hooked on the idea of the picture-perfect future that she'd stopped paying attention to the present, to whether or not Angus even made her happy.

The lift doors eased open silently, directly into a large living room. It took only a moment to realise they were on the top floor of the hotel and that this magnificent space must surely be the penthouse.

'Wow.' For a second, everything but admiration left her—this place was amazing. Every bit as decadent as the foyer but even more so because it was designed with a single occupant in mind. Everything was pale—cream, Scandinavian wood furniture, glass, mirrors, except for the artwork that was bold—a Picasso hung on one wall. There were plants, too, large fiddle-leaf figs that added a bold hint of architectural interest.

Sliding glass doors led to a balcony that showed a stunning view of Athens in the distance—glowing golden warm, an ancient city, so full of stories and interest.

'This is beautiful.'

He dipped his head in silent concession, moving towards the kitchen and pulling a bottle of champagne from the fridge. She recognised the label for its distinctive golden colour.

She watched as he unfurled the foil and popped the cork effortlessly, grabbing two flutes and half filling them.

'What brings you to Chrysá Vráchia, Hannah?'

There it was again, her name in his mouth, being kissed by his accent. Her knees felt shaky; she wasn't sure she trusted them to carry her across the room.

'A change,' she said cryptically. 'And you?'

His lips twisted and she felt something sharpen within him, something that sparked a thousand little questions inside her. 'It's routine. I come here every year.'

'What for?'

He didn't answer. Instead, he strode across the room, champagne flute in hand, passing Hannah's to her as though he were fighting himself, as though he were fighting this.

And she couldn't understand that.

If it weren't for the gale-force strength of her own needs, she might have paused to ask him why he was looking at her with such intensity, why he stared at her in a way that seemed to strip her soul bare.

But the incessant thrumming of her own desire was all Hannah was conscious of.

'Habit,' he said simply, swallowing so his Adam's apple bobbed in his throat.

She bit down on her lip, and his eyes dropped to her mouth, so her desire became louder, more urgent, desperation rolling through her. This was crazy. Madness. Necessary.

Outside, a spark of colour exploded through the sky—bright red, vibrant, its beauty an imperative they both resisted.

'Happy new year,' she said quietly, unable to take her eyes off his face.

Happy new year? He stared at the woman he'd brought up to his penthouse, completely at a loss for what the hell had come over him. For four years he'd come here to pay his respects to Amy, he'd undertaken this pilgrimage, he'd come here to remember her.

For four years he'd resisted any woman he found desirable, he'd ignored his body's hungers, he'd resisted anything except the debt he felt he owed Amy.

Then again, no other woman had ever slammed into his body. She had literally hit him out of nowhere, and the second his hand had curled around her arm, simply to steady her, his body had tightened with a whole raft of needs he no longer wanted to ignore.

He'd sworn he'd spend the rest of his life single, celibate.

Amy's.

But right here, with the starlit sky exploding beyond the glass wall of his penthouse apartment, something within him shifted. It was as though an ancient, unseen force was propelling him to act, was reminding him that grief could coexist with virility, that he could have sex with a woman without it being a betrayal to his wife.

He had loved Amy, even when their marriage had been fraught and neither of them particularly happy. She was his wife, he'd made a promise to her, and he had sworn he'd love only her for the rest of his life. So wasn't it loving another woman that was the true betrayal?

What did sex have to do with it?

No, denying his libido wasn't about what he owed Amy. It was punishment.

Punishment for being the son of a criminal mastermind. Punishment for being careless, for thinking he could turn his back on Dion Stathakis and live his life without the long, gnarled fingers of that man's sins reaching in and shredding what he, Leonidas, possessed.

He had been punishing himself because he deserved to feel that desperate pain of denial, that constant throbbing of need.

And he still should.

But there was something about Hannah that weakened his resolve to the point of breaking. He didn't believe in angels and ghosts, he didn't believe in fairy tales and myths, and yet, in that moment, it almost felt as if she'd been sent to him, a fragment of his soul, a promise that he could weaken, for one night, and go back to hating himself again tomorrow.

In the light of day, with the breaking of another year over this earth, he could resume his uneasy life.

But for tonight, or what was left of it, he could forget. With determination in his gaze, he put their champagne flutes down, knowing there was no turning back from this, no changing the immediate future.

'Happy new year.' And he dropped his head,

surprising her completely if her husky little gasp was anything to go by, parting her lips so he could drive his tongue deep inside her and feel every reverberation of her body, he could taste her desire and welcome it with his own.

Just for this night, he would be a slave to this—and then, everything could go back to normal…

CHAPTER TWO

PERHAPS SHE'D EXPECTED him to kiss her gently, to explore her slowly, but there was nothing gentle about this, nothing slow. It was a kiss of urgency and it detonated around them.

She made a groaning noise into his mouth, her desire roaring through her body, taking control of her.

This was not a warm, comfortable kiss. It was a kiss that redefined everything in her life, pushing new boundaries into place. She clung to his shirt for dear life and he kissed her deeper, his mouth moving over hers, demanding more of her, his tongue duelling with her own, his body cleaved to hers so not a breath of space remained between them.

It was a kiss of complete domination and she succumbed to it utterly.

'Just this one night.' He pushed the words into her mouth as he spun her body, tightening his arms around her waist and lifting her in his arms. He sat down on the sofa, pulling her onto his lap, pushing at her dress and making a guttural sound of frustration when he found the cotton of her underpants.

It was everything she wanted—the imperma-
nence, the perfect treatment. She wanted to lose
her virginity—it seemed ridiculous to be twenty-
three and not know what sex was all about, yet
the idea of a relationship made something inside
her shrivel up and die.

She'd never trust another man, she'd never
want love, or believe in love. She'd never be fool-
ish enough to believe *she* was lovable.

But sex?

This?

This was a balm to her soul.

She tilted her head back as he pushed her dress
higher, over her arms and then from her body altogether, so she wore only her underwear, flimsy
cotton, with no care whatsoever that this man
she'd met less than an hour ago was seeing her
like this.

If anything, she found her total abandon to
this—to him—liberating.

There was no room for any such rational con-
sideration, though, when he unhooked the bra
and discarded it carelessly, then began to trace
one of her nipples with his tongue, circling the
peach areola lightly at first, so she was trembling
on top of him, straddling his lap.

He moved his mouth closer to the tip of her
nipple and, finally, surrounded it completely,

sucking on her flesh in a way that burst starlight behind her eyes.

She swore, uncharacteristically, and he echoed it in his native tongue, reaching between her legs and pushing at the trousers of his designer suit, unzipping them, unbuttoning them so that the arousal she could feel through the material was hard and naked.

He transferred his mouth to her other breast and the first, so sensitive from his ministrations, felt the sting of the cool, air-conditioned air and she arched her back in response.

It was completely overwhelming.

Or, she thought it was. But then, he moved his hand between her legs and through the waistband of her underwear, sliding a finger into her moist core, and she cried his name.

He stilled for a moment then moved his finger deeper, finding her sensitive cluster of nerves and tormenting it until she was panting, desperate, so desperate, before pulling his finger out, fixing her with a look of wonderment.

'You are so wet.'

She was, and shaking all over, desire like an electrical current and it was frying her completely.

'I know,' she groaned as his hands moved to the top of her underpants and began to push at them. She shifted her body, lifting herself up so he could undress her completely, needing to be naked, needing him.

She had no experience but she had instincts and they were driving her wild, needing her to act, to feel, to do. She groaned as she stood shakily, naked before him, wanting to experience everything. There was a type of madness overtaking her, building within her.

She reached a hand out for his and he stood, wrapping his arms around her, crushing her to his frame.

'Who are you?' he groaned into her mouth, the words making no sense.

'Hannah,' she said unevenly and he laughed, a husky sound.

'Yes. But what kind of mermaid or angel or fairy are you to come here and do this to me?'

She swallowed his words, kissing him right back, her tongue duelling with his, passion making their breath harsh and loud in the still night air.

'Leonidas,' she groaned his name and his hands curved around her naked rear, lifting her up, wrapping her legs around his body as he strode through the penthouse towards what turned out to be a bedroom. It was huge with the same view towards Athens. He eased her down without bothering to turn on the lights so every sparkle of fireworks was like a jolt into the room.

Her hands tugged at his shirt with such desperation a button popped off and flew through the room.

She cursed softly under her breath, her eyes apologetic when they latched to his.

He shook his head. 'Don't worry.'

She nodded, but he finished the job, stripping the shirt from his body to reveal a broadly muscled chest that had her pulse ratcheting up yet another gear so she was almost trembling with the force of her own body's demands.

'Wow.' She stared at the ridges of his torso, transfixed by the obvious strength there, and lifted her hands to trace his abdominals almost without realising it. 'Work out much?'

She didn't see the way his lips flickered into a smile, nor could she have any idea how rare that smile was. Her hands ran down his chest, finding the waist of his pants and pushing at them, her eyes lifting to his as she sucked her lower lip between her teeth.

She was completely inexperienced and yet Hannah felt no anxiety, no nervousness, nothing except desire bursting through her, jolting her body as though she'd picked up a bundle of live wires.

'I want you,' she said, in awe of how true that was. It went beyond needing revenge on Angus, it went beyond anything to do with Angus. There was nothing and no one in Hannah's mind as she lifted onto the tips of her toes so she could claim Leonidas's mouth with her own, her kiss curious, questioning and then desperate.

He kissed her back, their bodies moulded together, desire a flame that was growing bigger than either could control. 'I want to take this slow,' he groaned, his hands tangling in her russet hair, curling it up and holding it against her head. He took a step forward, pushing her backwards until Hannah collapsed onto the bed, his body following, the weight and strength of him an impossible pleasure.

'I want this,' she said again, more to herself than him. 'Don't take it slow.'

He lifted himself up to stare at her, his eyes showing emotions she couldn't comprehend, or perhaps her ability to comprehend was blunted by the sheer force of her own feelings, which were overwhelming her, robbing her of sense and logic and reason.

'You don't know...'

His words were engulfed by her kiss. Hannah was sick of being patient; she was sick of waiting. She'd never known desire like this but that didn't mean she wasn't prepared to answer its call. 'Please,' she groaned. 'Make love to me.'

The words were breathed into his being, sparkling like the light show beyond the window.

Explosions of light, intense, glowing, hot. He separated her legs, nudging the tip of his arousal against her womanhood, and Hannah held her breath, she held everything.

For a split second, she contemplated telling him she was innocent, that she'd never done this before, but there was no time. He thrust into her and with her gasp he stilled, pushing up to stare down at her, his features harsh in the darkened room.

'*Theos*, Hannah, was that…were you?'

'Don't stop,' she said, shaking her head, but Leonidas was already pulling away from her, his body rock hard, his eyes pinning her with intensity. 'Please don't stop.' Her heart crumbled. She hadn't realised until that moment how desperately she wanted to know herself to be desirable. To know that someone wanted her enough to be unable to control their desire.

He swore under his breath and moved to the night stand, sliding open the drawer and pulling out a foil square. 'Not once have I forgotten protection,' he said thickly, the words coated in his own desires, which began to put Hannah's heart back together again.

She watched as he unfurled a condom over his length then came back to the bed, his body weight returning to hers, bliss fogging into her mind.

'You should have told me.' The words lacked

recrimination. They were simple. Soft. Gentle. Enquiring. As if he was asking her to assure him she was okay.

'I didn't know how.'

'I'm a virgin?'

She laughed, despite the desire that was pulling at her gut. 'I was a virgin.'

'You are sure this is what you want?'

She nodded, lifting her hands up to cup his face. 'Please.'

But he didn't respond. Something tightened in his expression, his jaw moving as though he were grinding his teeth. 'I meant what I said, Hannah. One night. Nothing more.'

'I know that.' She nodded, thinking of the situation she'd left behind, the mess her private life was in. The last thing she wanted was the complication of more than one night.

And it was the freedom he needed, the reassurance he obviously craved, because he pushed back into her. Gently this time, slowly, giving her time to adjust and adapt, allowing her inexperienced body a chance to get used to this invasion, to feel his presence and relish in it before taking more of her, more of her, until finally she was crying his name over and over, the foreign syllables tripping off her tongue as rushed breaths filled her lungs.

His mouth moved from hers to her cheek then

lower to the sensitive flesh at the base of her neck, his tongue flicking her pulse point while his hands roamed her body, feeling every inch of her, pausing where she responded loudest to his inquisition, teasing the sensitive flesh of her breasts, tormenting her nipples with the skill of his hands.

It was heaven.

Pleasure built inside Hannah like a coil winding tighter and tighter and she dug her nails into his back, moaning softly as the spring prepared to burst. She arched her back and rolled her head to the side, the fireworks gaining momentum as her own pleasure began to detonate. She lifted her hips in a silent, knowing invitation and he held her, his hands keeping her close to him, reassuring her as she lost herself utterly to the compelling, indescribable pleasure of a sexual orgasm.

It was intense and it was fast and it robbed her of breath and control. Her eyelids filled with light, her mouth tasted like steel. She pushed up on her elbows, staring into Leonidas's eyes, feeling quite mad and delirious with what she'd just experienced.

But it was nowhere near over.

He braced himself above her on his palms, watching the play of sensation on her features, and then he began to move again, his body stirring hers to new heights, his dominance something that made her want to weep.

She knew though, instinctively, that giving into the salty tang of tears would be a bad idea. Even while she was part mad with pleasure, she didn't want to show how completely he'd shifted something inside her, nor how much this meant to her.

Because Hannah felt a surge of feminine power and it was instantaneous and went beyond words. She didn't need to tell him how much this meant to her; she felt it and that was enough.

Angus had made her feel precious and valued, he'd made her feel like an *objet d'art* and that had been nice. It had been better than knowing herself to be an unwanted nuisance, which was how she'd spent a huge portion of her childhood since the loss of her parents. But he'd never looked at her as though he would die if he didn't kiss her.

He'd never looked at her as though the push and pull of their chemistry was robbing him of sense.

Leonidas was, though.

He moved his body and he stared into her eyes and she felt a cascade of emotions from him to her and none of them would be worth analysing, because this was just one night. A temporary, fleeting, brief night—a slice out of time.

* * *

Sitting on the edge of the bed, Leonidas cradled his head in his hands, staring at the floor between his feet. Early dawn light was peeking through the window. Hannah's rhythmic breathing filled the room, soft and somehow sweet. Sweet? How could breath be sweet? He turned to face her on autopilot, his expression grim.

He didn't know how, but it was.

She was sweet.

She'd been innocent.

He cursed silently, standing and pulling his pants on, watching her through a veil of disbelief. What the hell had come over him? Four years of celibacy and then he'd spontaneously combusted the second the beautiful redhead had literally bumped into him?

And it wasn't the red hair, nor the passing resemblance to Amy. If anything, that would have been a reason to keep his distance. No, this was something else. A kind of sexual starvation that he supposed was only natural, given he'd denied himself this pleasure and release for such a long time. But, *Theos*, a virgin?

He hadn't wanted that! He had wanted meaningless, empty sex. A quick roll in the hay to satisfy this part of him, to obliterate his grief, to remind him that he was a man, a breathing, living man with blood in his veins.

And instead, he'd taken a young woman's innocence. He'd been her first.

A sense of disbelief filled him as he watched her sleeping, her gentle inhalations, her lips that were tilted into a smile even in her sleep.

He'd always be her first. No matter what happened, no matter who she slept with, he was that to her.

It wasn't meaningless; it never could be. Thank God he'd remembered protection. He'd have put money on the fact she wasn't on birth control—why would she be? He could think of nothing worse than that kind of consequence from a night of unplanned pleasure.

And it had been a night of pleasure, he thought with a strong lurch of desire in his gut. Despite her inexperience, she had matched him perfectly, her body answering every call of his, her inquisitiveness driving him wild, the way she'd kissed and licked her way over his frame, tasting all of him, experimenting with what pleased him, asking him to tell her what he needed.

He groaned, a quiet noise but she stirred, shifting a little, so the sheet fell down and revealed her pert, rounded breasts to his gaze.

His erection throbbed against his pants. He took a step back from the bed.

One night, and dawn was breathing its way

through the room, reminding him that this was not his life.

Hannah was an aberration. A mistake.

He had to leave. He had to forget this ever happened. He just hoped she would, too.

Hannah woke slowly, her body delightfully sore, muscles she hadn't felt before stretching inside her as she shifted, rolling onto her side.

A Cavalcanti masterpiece was on the wall opposite, the morning light bathing its modernist palette in gold, a gold she knew would be matched by the sheer cliffs of this spectacular island.

But none of these things were what she wanted to see most.

She flipped over, her eyes scanning the bed, looking for Leonidas. He wasn't there.

She reached out, feeling the sheets. They were cold. Her stomach grumbled and she pushed to sitting, smothering a yawn with the back of her hand. When had they finally fallen asleep? She couldn't remember.

A smile played about her lips as she stood, grabbing the sheet and wrapping it toga style around her, padding through the penthouse.

'Leonidas?' She frowned, looking around. The glass doors to the balcony were open. She moved towards it, the view spectacular, momentarily robbing her of breath for a wholly new reason.

He wasn't out there.

She frowned, turning on her heel and heading back inside. It was then that she saw it.

A note.

And there was so much to comprehend in that one instant that she struggled to make sense of any of it.

First of all the letterhead. It was no standard issue hotel notepad. It bore the insignia of the hotel, but the embossed lettering at the bottom spelled 'Leonidas Stathakis.'

Leonidas Stathakis? Her heart began to race faster as she comprehended this. She didn't know much about the Stathakis brothers—she wasn't really *au fait* with people of their *milieu*, but no one could fail to have at least *heard* of the Stathakis brothers. To know that they were two of the richest men in the world. There were other facts, too, swirling just beneath the surface. Snatches she'd heard or read but not paid attention to because it had all seemed so far away. Crimes? The mob? Murder? Was that them? Or someone else?

She swallowed, running her finger over the embossing, closing her eyes and picturing Leonidas as he'd been the night before. As he'd stood so close to her and their eyes had seemed to pierce one another's souls.

Her pulse gushed and she blinked her green eyes open, scanning the paper more thoroughly this time, expecting to see a few lines explaining that he'd gone to get breakfast, or for a workout—those muscles didn't just grow themselves—or something along those lines.

What she wasn't expecting was the formality and finality of what she read.

Hannah
It shouldn't have happened. Please forget it did. The penthouse is yours for as long as you'd like it.
Leonidas

She read it and reread it at least a dozen times, her fingers shaking as she reached for the coffee machine and jabbed the button. Outrage warred with anger.

It shouldn't have happened.

Because she hadn't been what he'd expected? Because she hadn't been any good?

Oh, God.

Was it possible that the desire she'd felt had been one-sided? Angus had been engaged to her and been able to easily abstain from sex, yet he'd been fooling around behind her back.

Had she been a let-down?

Hurt flooded inside her, disbelief echoing in her heart.

She'd wanted to come to Chrysá Vráchia almost her whole life, but suddenly, she couldn't wait to leave.

CHAPTER THREE

A WEEK AFTER leaving the island, Leonidas awoke in a cold sweat. He stared around the hotel room, his heart hammering in his chest.

Hannah.

He'd been dreaming of Hannah, the woman he'd met on Chrysá Vráchia. He'd been dreaming of her, of making love to her. His body was rock hard and he groaned, falling back onto the pillows, closing his eyes and forcing himself to breathe slowly, to calm down. To remember his wife.

And nausea skidded through him, because he knew he would never forget Amy. But for those few moments, when he'd lost himself inside Hannah, when he'd pierced her innocence, and possessed her so completely, he had felt…

He had felt like himself.

For the first time in many years he had felt like a man who was free of this curse, this guilt, this permanent ache.

He had lost himself in Hannah and, just for a moment, he had lost his grief.

He swore under his breath, and pushed the sheet back, his heart unable to be calmed. Leonidas walked to the plush kitchen of his Hong Kong penthouse, pressing a button on the coffee machine.

He watched it brew, an answering presentiment of disaster growing inside him.

'Do you need me to talk to him?'

Leonidas focussed on sounding normal. But in the month since leaving Chrysá Vráchia, he'd had a growing tension, balling in his gut, and nothing he did seemed to relieve it. It was guilt, he knew. Guilt at having betrayed his vows to Amy. At having broken the vow he made himself, that Amy would be the last woman he was intimate with.

The limousine slid through Rome, lights on either side.

'Yeah, sure, that's even better,' Thanos responded with sarcasm. Leonidas's younger brother shook his head. 'Kosta Carinedes will take one look at you and see Dad. Sorry.'

Leonidas winced—the physical similarities between himself and Dion were not news to him. 'So how are you going to convince him to sell?'

'He wants to sell,' Thanos murmured, tilting his head as the car slowed at a corner and paused near a group of beautiful women wearing skimpy shorts and singlet tops. 'He just doesn't want to sell to us.'

'Because of Dion?'

'Because of our name,' Thanos conceded with a nod. 'And because I am, quote, "a sex-mad bachelor".'

At this, Leonidas laughed, despite the bad mood that had been following him for weeks. 'He's got you bang to rights there.'

Thanos grinned. 'Hey, I don't think there's anything wrong with being sex-mad. We can't all live the life of a saint like you.'

Leonidas's expression shifted as though he'd been punched in the gut. He was far more sinner than saint, but he had no intention of sharing his slip-up with his brother.

'Offer him more money,' Leonidas suggested, cutting to the crux of the matter.

'It's not about money. This is his grandparents' legacy. They built the company out of "love",' he said the word with sardonic derision, 'and he won't sell it to someone who's constantly in the headlines for all the wrong reasons.'

Leonidas shrugged. 'Then let it go.'

'You're kidding, right? I told you what this means to me? And who else is interested in buying it?'

Leonidas regarded his brother thoughtfully. 'Yes. Luca Monato. And I know you two hate each other. But this is just a company. Let him have it, buy its competition and drive him into the ground. Far more satisfying.'

'It might come to that. But I'm not done yet.'

'What else can you do? I hate to point out the obvious, but Kosta's right. You're a man whore, Thanos.'

Thanos laughed. 'And proud. You could take a couple of pages out of my book. In fact, why don't you? I've got a heap of women you'd like. Why don't you call one of them? Take her for dinner and then back to your place…'

Leonidas turned away from his brother, looking out of the window of the limousine as Rome passed in a beautiful, dusk-filled blur. He thought of Hannah, his body tightening, his chest feeling as if it were filling with acid. 'No.'

'You cannot live the rest of your life like this,' Thanos insisted quietly, his tone serious now, their banter forgotten. There weren't many people on earth who could speak plainly to the great Leonidas Stathakis, but Thanos was one of them, and always had been. Side by side they'd dealt with their father's failings, his criminality, his convictions, the ruin he'd brought on their fortune and the Stathakis name.

Side by side, they'd rebuilt it all, better than before, returning their family's once-great wealth— many times over. They were half-brothers, only three months apart in age, and they'd been raised more as twins since Thanos was abandoned on their doorstep by his mother at the age of eight. Their insight into one another was unique.

Leonidas understood Thanos as nobody else did, and vice versa. Leonidas knew what it had done to Thanos, his mother abandoning him, choosing to desert him rather than find a way to manage his dominant character traits.

'What would you do?' Leonidas drawled, but there was tension in the question. Tension and despair.

Thanos expelled a sigh; the car stopped. Thousands of screaming fans were outside on the red carpet, here to catch a glimpse of the A-list Hollywood stars who'd featured in the film of the premiere they were attending.

'I can't say. I get it—you miss Amy. What happened to her and Brax—do you think I don't feel that? You think I don't want to reach into that prison cell and strangle our father with my bare hands for what he exposed you to? But, Leonidas, you cannot serve her by living half a life. Do you think Amy would have wanted this for you?'

Leonidas swept his dark eyes shut, the panic in his gut churning, the sense of self-disgust almost impossible to manage. 'Don't.' He shook his head. 'Do not speak to me of Amy's wishes.'

But Thanos wasn't to be deterred. 'She loved

you. She would want you to live the rest of your life as you did before. Be happy. Be fulfilled.'

'You think I deserve that?'

'It was our father's crimes that killed her, not yours.'

'But if she hadn't met me…' Leonidas insisted, not finishing the statement—not needing to. Thanos knew; he understood.

'It's been four years,' Thanos repeated softly. 'You have mourned and grieved and honoured them both. It's time to move forward.'

But Leonidas shook his head, his time on Chrysá Vráchia teaching him one thing and one thing only: it would never be time. He had failed Amy during their marriage, in many ways; he wouldn't fail her now.

'Tuna salad, please,' Hannah said over the counter, scanning the lunch selections with a strange sense of distaste, despite the artful arrangements. In the four months since arriving in London and taking up a maternity-leave contract as legal secretary to a renowned litigator, Hannah had grabbed lunch from this same store almost every day.

Her boss liked the chicken sandwiches and she the tuna. She waited in the queue then grabbed their lunches and made her way back to the office as quickly as she could.

There was a wait for the lift and she stifled a yawn, sipping her coffee. Her stomach flipped. She frowned. The milk tasted funny.

'Great,' she said with a sigh, dropping it into a waste bin. Just what she needed—spoiled milk.

But when she got to her desk and unpeeled her sandwich, she had the strangest sense that she might vomit. She took one bite of the sandwich and then stood up, rushing to the facilities. She just made it.

It was as she hovered over the porcelain bowl, trying to work out whether she was sick or suffering from food poisoning, that dates began to hover in her mind. Months of dates, in fact, without her regular cycle.

Her skin was damp with perspiration as she straightened, staring at the tiled wall with a look of absolute shock.

No way.

No way could she be pregnant. Her hand curved over her stomach—it was still flat. Except her jeans had felt tight on the weekend, and she'd put it down to the sedentary job.

But what if it wasn't just a little weight gain? What if she was growing thick around the midsection because she was carrying Leonidas Stathakis's baby?

She gasped audibly, pushing out of the cubicle,

and ran the taps, staring at herself in the mirror as the ice water ran over her fingertips.

Surely it wasn't true? It was just a heap of co-incidences. She had a tummy bug and her weight gain *was* attributable to the fact she was chained to a desk for twelve-hour days. That could also account for her recent exhaustion.

That was all.

Nonetheless, when she left the office much later that day, still feeling unwell, Hannah ducked into a pharmacy around the corner from the Earl's Court flat she'd rented a room in.

She'd do a pregnancy test. There was no harm in that—it was a simple precaution.

In the privacy of her the bathroom, she un-sealed the box, read the instructions, and did pre-cisely what they said. She set an alarm on her phone, to tell her when two minutes was up.

She didn't need it, though.

It took fewer than twenty seconds for a second line to appear.

A strong, vibrant pink, showing that she was, indeed, pregnant.

With Leonidas Stathakis's baby.

'Oh, jeez.' She sat down on the toilet lid, and stared at the back of the door. Her hand curved over her stomach and she closed her eyes. His face appeared in her mind, unbidden, unwanted, and unflinchingly and just as he had been for months in her dreams, she saw him naked, his strong body and handsome face so close to her that she could breathe him in, except he was just a phantom, a ghost.

But not for long.

It shouldn't have happened. Despite the fact she'd torn his note into a thousand pieces and left it scattered over the marble bench-top of the luxurious penthouse kitchen, his words were indelibly imprinted into her mind.

Well, regardless of his regret, and the fact he hadn't respected her enough to say that to her face, she'd have to see him again.

There was nothing for it—she had to face this reality, to tell him the truth.

And she would—when she was ready.

Hannah checked the name against the piece of paper she clutched in her hand, looking around the marina with a frown on her face.

There was some event on, Capri Sailing Week or some such, and the whole marina was bursting with life. Enormous boats—or 'superyachts', as she'd been told they were called—lined up like swans, so graceful and imposing in the evening sun.

She knew from the search she'd done on the Internet that Stathakis Corp owned a boat that took part in the event. She also knew that Leonidas and his brother came to the event annually on their own 'superyacht'. Photos had shown her a suntanned Leonidas relaxing on the deck, casting his eye over the race.

She'd closed out of the images as quickly as she could.

She didn't need to see him again. Not like that.

This was going to be quick, like ripping off a plaster. She'd tell him she was pregnant—not that she'd really need words. At more than five months along, she was quite visibly carrying a baby.

She'd been so tempted just to call him. To deliver the news over the phone and leave it at that, just as he'd written her a note instead of having the courage to face her the next morning.

But it was cowardly and she wasn't that. They were having a baby together—she couldn't ignore the ramifications of their night together and nor could he. At least she knew that, no matter what happened next, he'd regretted that night.

He'd regretted it, he wished that it hadn't happened, and he'd treated her with complete disdain and disrespect, skulking out in the middle of the night, leaving a note! It wasn't as if she'd have begged him for more—they'd both agreed to it being one night only. It was the salt in the wound of him vanishing, not even bothering to say goodbye.

That was the man she was having a child with.

She grabbed hold of that thought; she needed to remember that.

The Stathakis yacht was the biggest in the marina, and it was pumping with life and noise. Her eyes skimmed the yacht, running over the partygoers moving around with effortless grace, all scantily clad, from what she could see. Music with a heavy beat sounded loud and somehow seductive, so something began to beat low in her abdomen. There were staff, too, their crisp white shirts discernible even at a distance, the trays they carried overflowing with champagne flutes.

She narrowed her eyes, lifting a hand and wiping it over her forehead. She was warm—the sun was beating down, even now in the early evening, and she'd been travelling since that morning.

She was tired, too, the exhaustion of the first trimester not giving way in the second.

She moved closer to the yacht, mindful on her approach that security guards stood casually at the bridge that led to the deck.

As she approached, one of the men spoke to her in Italian. At her blank expression, he switched to Greek and then, finally, English. 'Can I help you, miss?'

'I need to see Leonidas Stathakis. It's important.'

The security guard flicked his gaze over

Hannah, his expression unchanging. 'It's a private party.'

She had expected this resistance. 'If you tell him my name, I'm certain he'll want to see me.'

The guard's scepticism was obvious. 'And that is?'

'Hannah. Hannah May.' Her voice was soft, her Australian accent prominent.

The guard spoke into his walkie-talkie, the background noise of the party coming through louder when he clicked the button at its side. She discerned only her own name in the rapid delivery of information. Then, he clicked the walkie-talkie back to his hip.

'He says you can go up.'

'Thank you.'

Nerves were jangling inside her, doubts firing in her gut. Maybe she should turn around. Go back to London, or even Australia, far away. Call him with this information. Or not. She had no idea. She just knew suddenly the thought of coming face-to-face with Leonidas filled her with ice.

She was going to be sick.

'Miss? Are you okay?'

But she'd come all this way. She'd grappled with this for weeks now, she'd faced the reality of being pregnant with Leonidas's baby, trying to work out the best way to tell him. She had to tell him—there was nothing for it.

'I will be.'

Yes, she would be. She needed simply to get this over with. The faster the better. 'This way?' she prompted, gesturing towards the boat.

'And to the left.'

Hannah's smile was tight as she surveyed the crowd, not particularly relishing the idea of weaving her way through so many people. 'Thank you.'

She stepped onto a platform and then went up a set of polished timber and white stairs. At the top, another guard opened a section of the boat's balustrade, forming a gate. The noise was deafening up here. She braced herself for a moment, frozen to the spot as she recognised at least a dozen Hollywood celebrities walking around in a state of undress. Men, women, all in their bathers, suntanned, impossibly slender and toned with very white teeth and enormous eyes.

Hannah stared at them self-consciously, this world so foreign to her, so foreign to anything and anyone she knew. These people were his friends?

There was a loud noise, a laugh, and then the splashing of water. She turned, chasing the interruption, to see a handsome man standing above the pool, a grin on his chiselled face. It wasn't Leonidas, but she recognised him nonetheless from the few photos she'd pulled up while trying to find out how to contact Leonidas.

Thanos Stathakis, the playboy prince of Europe, all golden and carefree, and surrounded by a dozen women who were quite clearly vying for a place in his bed. She pulled a face, straightened her spine and began to cut through the party.

She didn't belong here. She didn't want to be here. She just needed to tell him and get out.

'Miss May?' A woman wearing a crew uniform approached Hannah, a professional smile on her pretty face. 'This way, please.'

Hannah nodded stiffly, falling into step beside the woman, almost losing her footing when she saw a Grammy award–winning singer breeze past, laughing, arm in arm with the undisputed queen of talk-show television.

Hannah stared after them, her heart pounding. She felt like a fish way, way out of water. The crew member pushed a door open and Hannah followed, grateful for the privacy and quiet the room afforded.

'Would you like anything to drink, miss?'

Hannah shook her head. 'No, thank you.'

She waited until she was alone and then scanned the room, her eyes taking in the obvious signs of wealth that were littered without care. The yacht was unlike anything she'd ever seen, the last word in luxury and money. Designer furniture filled out this room, a television the size of her bed on one wall, and through the glass partition a huge bedroom with a spa against the windows.

Leonidas's bedroom?

Her pulse picked up a notch and on autopilot she wandered towards it, her heart hammering against her chest as she pushed the door open.

Yes. She couldn't say how she knew, only there was something in the air, his masculine, alpine fragrance that instantly jolted her senses.

She backed out quickly, as though the very fires of hell were lining the floor in there.

She had to do this. She would tell him, and then leave, giving him a chance to digest it, and to consider her wishes. This would be over in minutes.

Minutes.

She waited, and with each moment that passed her nerves stretched tighter, thinner, finer and more tremulous, so, five minutes later, she honestly thought she might pass out.

She was on the brink of leaving the room and going in search of Leonidas herself when the door burst inwards and he strode into the room, wearing only a pair of swimming shorts, and a look that—in the seconds before surprise contorted his expression—showed his impatience with her arrival.

He was partying.

He was probably the centre of attention, being

just as fawned over and celebrated as his brother. Jealousy tore through her, but Hannah told herself it was outrage. Outrage that she'd been agonising over the baby they were going to have while he'd slipped out of bed and gone back to his normal life as though it had never happened.

If she'd held even a single shred of hope that he might be glad to see her, it disappeared immediately.

'Hannah.' His eyes roamed her face and then dropped lower, until he was staring at her stomach, and she felt the force of his shock, the reverberation of his confusion. It slammed into the room, slammed against her, and if she weren't so consumed with her own feelings she might almost have felt sympathy for him.

'Yes.' She answered the unspoken question, her voice slightly shaky. 'I'm pregnant. And you're the father.'

CHAPTER FOUR

HIS EYES SWEPT SHUT, almost as if he could wipe this meeting from reality, as if he would open his gaze and she'd be gone. It wasn't until that moment Hannah realised that she'd been partly hoping he would react well to this news. While neither of them had planned this, nor wanted it particularly, a baby was still cause for celebration, wasn't it?

Apparently not.

When he opened his eyes and his gaze pierced her soul, it was with a look of rejection, and panic.

'No.' He glared at her. 'This cannot be happening.'

Hannah curved a hand around her stomach, trying to be generous, to remember he was shocked, that she'd had time to adjust to this news and he was being presented with it all now.

'Really?' She arched a brow, her obvious pregnant state contradicting that.

He swore in his native tongue and moved towards a bar in the corner, pulling out two bottles of mineral water. He stalked towards her and held one out and she took it without thinking, her fingers curving over the top.

But, oh, she was so close to him now, and the last five months disappeared, everything disappeared, except this wave of intense recognition and need, that same spark of hunger that had incinerated her on New Year's Eve.

Her breath escaped her on a hiss; she stood frozen to the spot, her eyes glued to his, her face tilted upwards, her body on alert for his nearness. It was an instant, visceral, physical reaction and it shook her to the core.

But even before her eyes, Leonidas's surprise was giving way to comprehension. His jaw tightened and he nodded slowly, releasing the water bottle into her grip and stepping away from her, turning to stare at the ocean.

'How do you feel?'

She was surprised by the question—she hadn't expected it, this rapid assimilation of information, acceptance and then a hint of civility.

'I'm mostly okay.' She nodded, opening the bottle and taking a sip gratefully. 'I'm quite tired but otherwise fine.'

He didn't react. 'Do you know what gender it is?'

Hannah nodded again, but he wasn't looking. 'Yes.' She reached into her handbag, her fingers fumbling a little as she lifted out an ultrasound picture. 'Here.'

At that word, he turned slowly, his expression

grim, his gaze lowering to the flimsy black and white photograph. He made no effort to take it.

'It's a girl,' she said quietly.

He still didn't reach for the picture, but his eyes swept shut as though he were steeling himself against this, as though it wasn't what he wanted. Hurt scored her being. But before she could fire that accusation at him, he was shooting another question at her.

'When did you find out?'

She swallowed in an attempt to bring moisture back to her dry throat. 'A while ago,' she admitted.

'When?'

A hint of guilt flared in her gut but she reminded herself she'd done nothing wrong.

'I've known for a few weeks.'

He stared at her, long and hard, for several moments. 'You didn't think I deserved to know when you did?'

She shook her head once, from one side to the other. 'You didn't think I deserved more than to wake up to a crummy note?'

He froze, completely still, and the sound of the glamorous party outside the room thumped and crashed. Hannah didn't move. She glared at him, waiting for his answer.

It came swiftly, his brow furrowing. 'So this was payback? Retaliation of some kind?'

She shook her head. 'What? No. It was nothing like that.' She sucked in a breath, not wanting to be dragged off topic. 'I just wanted a chance to get used to this before I had to deal with you.'

'And you are now used to it?' he demanded, heat in the question.

She let out a small laugh, but it was a sound completely without humour. 'I'm not sure I'll ever adjust.'

'I don't want anything from you, Leonidas,' she said firmly, not registering the way something like admiration sparked in his eyes. 'I had no idea who you were that night, nor that you're worth a squillion dollars. I have no interest in asking you for any kind of support payment or whatever.' She shuddered in rejection of the very idea.

'I mean it. This isn't my way of asking you to support me in any way. I don't want that.'

He spoke then, his voice low and husky. 'So what do you want?'

She bit down on her lip then immediately stopped when he took a step closer, his eyes on the gesture, his body seemingly pulled towards hers.

'I want…to know you'll be a part of her life,' she said quietly, her own childhood a black hole in her mind, swallowing her up. She would do whatever she could to make sure her own daughter never had to live with the grief she'd felt.

He was quiet, watching her, and nervousness fired in Hannah's gut. 'Don't misunderstand me,' she said thickly. 'I would happily never see you again. But our daughter deserves to know both her parents.' She lifted a hand, toying with the necklace she wore, running her finger over the chain distractedly. Hannah needed the security of knowing their child would have two people who loved her, two people in case something happened to one of them.

'I appreciate this news is probably an even bigger inconvenience to you than it was to me,' she said simply. 'I understand you didn't want this. You were very clear about that.' She cleared her throat, sidestepping him and moving towards the windows that framed a sensational view of the waters off the coast of Capri. 'But we are having a child together, and I don't want her to grow up thinking she's not wanted.' Hannah's voice cracked and she closed her eyes, sucking in breath, needing strength.

'You want me to be a part of our daughter's life?'

'Yes.' The word rushed out of her. She spun around, surprised to find Leonidas had come to stand right behind her, his eyes on hers, his expression impossible to comprehend.

'And what kind of part?'

She furrowed her brow, not understanding.

'Tell me, do you expect me to see her once a year? At Christmas, perhaps? Or for her birthdays, as well? Do you envisage I will spend time with my daughter according to a stopwatch?'

Hannah's eyes rounded in her face. 'I don't understand…'

'No,' he said succinctly and now she understood what was holding his face so completely still. He was angry!

'I will not be a figment of my child's life—the kind of father who exists like a tiny part of her.'

Hannah didn't get a chance to reassure him.

'My child will be raised by me.' His eyes were like flints of coal as he spoke. 'She will be raised with my name, and will have everything I can provide her with. She will be *mine*.'

At the completely possessive tone to his voice Hannah shuddered, because it was exactly how she felt, and they couldn't both raise their daughter.

'Don't make me regret coming here,' Hannah said quietly.

At this, his features grew taut, his jaw locked and his eyes showed a swirling comprehension that filled her with ice. 'Are you saying you contemplated not doing so?'

She paled, tilting her chin with a hint of rebellion. 'I've contemplated a great many things since I found out about her.'

'And was not telling me that I fathered a child one of those things you considered?'

Her cheeks glowed pink, revealing the truth of that statement. 'Briefly,' she conceded. 'Yes, of course. Wouldn't it be easier that way?'

Fury contorted his features and she rolled her eyes.

'I contemplated it for about three seconds before realising I could never do that. Obviously you deserve to know you're going to be a father. She's your child. I'm not saying you don't have a claim on her. But she's an innocent in this, she doesn't deserve to be pulled between us just because of that night.'

'I do not intend for her to be pulled between us.' He seized on this and, for a moment, she felt relief. Perhaps he was going to be reasonable after all, and not make this so difficult.

'You can be *very* involved,' she promised. 'I'm a reasonable person, Leonidas, and what I want most in this world is for our daughter to grow up secure in the love of her parents. But I want full custody. Full rights.' He didn't speak and she took strength from that. 'It's better this way, don't you see that?'

'Better for you,' he drawled, and then shook

his head angrily. 'At least, you seem to think it is, but you do not have all the facts, Hannah.'

'No? What am I missing?'

He ground his teeth together. 'Does it not occur to you that there are risks to you, to her, in being connected to someone like me?'

She blinked, and something tapped the back of her mind, something she'd seen on an Internet search. Only she'd tried not to look too deeply at his life, his past—she'd felt dirty enough having to look him up on the internet to find the name of this boat.

'No one needs to know.'

His laugh was a mocking snort. 'That's simplistic and naïve. The tabloid press probably already has paparazzi on your trail. That's before you show up to this—one of the most hotly photographed events of the year—heavily pregnant and asking to see me.'

'I am not heavily pregnant,' she said, and then clamped her mouth shut in frustration and the sheer irrelevancy of that. 'And so what? Who cares? Lots of people have illegitimate children. There'll be a rumour. We'll say nothing, and then it will die down.'

'You are missing my point,' he insisted darkly. 'From the minute this news hits the public domain, you will become a part of my world, and so will she, whether you want to be or not. Thinking you can just hide away from that is unrealistic.'

'So?' she said, though she hadn't considered this, and didn't particularly like the way it made her feel. 'I'll cope.'

'As a bare minimum, you will find yourself and your every move open to speculation in the gossip papers, and our daughter will be photographed and written about even when doing the most mundane things. You will want my protection from this, Hannah, and she will certainly deserve it.'

'I'd rather find my own way to protect her,' Hannah said crisply. 'I can handle a few photographers, and as for the stories, I just won't read them.'

His smile was a grim flicker of his lips. 'Sure, give that a go.' It was pure sarcasm.

'In any event, it is not,' he continued, 'the photographers that I am concerned with.'

She waited, holding a hand protectively over her stomach without realising it.

'I was married once,' he said, finally, the words like steel.

She remembered. Oh, it had been buried deep inside her mind, but as soon as he said it she recalled reading that, somewhere, at some time.

'And my wife was murdered.'

Hannah sucked in a gasp, sympathy pushing every other emotion from her mind.

'As was my two-year-old son.'

Hannah was hot and cold, sorrow and pain shooting through her. She almost felt as though she might faint.

'They were murdered as a vendetta against my father.' The words were strained and urgent. 'They lost their lives to hurt him and punish him. They were killed because of who they were to Dion Stathakis, and to me. I will not let that happen again. I will not let that happen to our daughter.'

Hannah's chest hurt. She'd known she was pregnant for a few weeks and already she knew she would give her life for this baby. She couldn't imagine the desperate agony of losing a toddler, of knowing a toddler to have met such a violent end.

'I'm so sorry.' The words were thick with tears. 'That must have been unbearable.' She swallowed, but the tears she was so adept at fighting filled her eyes.

He didn't respond—what could he say?

'But isn't that even more reason for me to hide away? To let me move far away from you and your world?'

'You cannot hide her. Not from men like him.'

A shiver ran down Hannah's spine.

'Only I can protect you both.'

Fear made Hannah tactless. 'I beg to differ, given the past...'

His expression cracked with pain and she winced.

'I'm so sorry. That was an awful thing to say. It's just...'

'No, you're right.' He held up a hand to stall her. 'I did not appreciate the danger to Amy and Brax. I failed them.' His voice was deep and her heart ached. 'I had no idea they were being watched, nor that a madman would use them to seek revenge on my father. His conviction did much damage to our business, and my brother and I worked tirelessly to make amends there, to return Stathakis Corp to its position of global prominence. That was my focus.

'I failed them, my wife and child, and I will never forget that, nor forgive myself.'

He straightened, his expression like iron. 'I will not make that mistake with her.'

He moved closer to Hannah, and she held her breath.

His hands curved over her stomach and she felt so much in that moment. It was as though a piece of string were wrapping from him to her, binding them, tying them together. If this had been a wedding ceremony it would have felt like a lesser commitment.

He focussed all his attention on Hannah. 'I will put everything I am into protecting you both, into ensuring men like that cannot get you. I cannot let you get on with your life as though this is simply an aberration when there may very well be a target over her head. Or yours, just because you happened to make the regrettable decision of sleeping with me one night.'

'You were the one who regretted it,' she pointed out and then shook her head, because that didn't matter any more. Panic was surging inside her; she felt as though she were falling back into a well only there was no light at the top of it.

She sucked in a breath but it burned through her lungs. 'Leonidas,' she groaned. 'I don't want anything to happen to her.'

'I won't let it,' he promised, lifting his hands to her face, holding her steady for his inspection. 'I promise you that.'

'How can you stop it?'

His eyes roamed her face intently. 'I will protect you and our daughter with my dying breath, that is how.'

She shook her head, the madness of this incongruous with the sounds of revelry beyond the room. Fear had her forgetting everything they were to one another, the brevity of their affair, his quickness to leave her, the fact he'd intended for them never to see one another again—and she'd agreed to that. In that moment, he was her lifeline, and she lifted a hand to his chest to take hold of it.

'Do you really think we're in danger?'

His eyes held hers and she felt the battle raging within him—a desire to reassure and placate her and a need to be honest.

'I will make sure you are not. But you must do what I say, and trust me to know what is right for you, for her, for our family.'

Family.

The word seemed to tear through both of them in different ways, each reacting to the emotion of that word, the harsh implications of such a term.

He looked stricken and Hannah felt completely shocked. She hadn't had a family in a long time. And even though this had been foisted on both of them, the word felt warm and loaded with promise. She swallowed past a lump in her throat and shook her head, nothing making sense.

'How? What? Tell me, Leonidas. I need to know she'll be okay.'

'Marry me,' he said simply, the words like rocks dropping into the boat.

'What?'

'Marry me, as soon as is legally possible.'

She sucked in a breath, his words doing strange things to her. In a thousand years, she hadn't expected this, and she had no way of processing how she felt. Marriage? To Leonidas Stathakis?

'How the heck is that going to help?'

'You'll be my wife, under my protection, living in my home. We will be raising our child together.'

The picture he painted was so seductive. Hannah took a fortifying breath, trying to disentangle the irrational desire to make sure her daughter didn't suffer the same miserable upbringing as she had from what was actually the *right* decision. It was impossible to think clearly.

Hannah shook her head slowly. 'It would never work between us.'

'What is there to "work"?' he asked simply. 'You love our child, do you not?'

Hannah's eyes sparked with his. 'With all my heart.'

'And you want to do what is best for her?'

Hannah's chin tilted in silent agreement.

'So trust me. Trust me to protect you both, to ensure her safety. I will never let anything happen to either of you.'

She nodded, listening to his words, hearing the intent in them.

'I cannot have my daughter raised anywhere but in my home,' he murmured, clearing his throat. She jerked her gaze to his and the depth of feeling in his eyes almost tore her in two.

'I need to *know* she is safe. That you are safe.'
He turned away from her, stalking towards the
table. He placed his palms on it, staring straight
ahead, out into the water. The party raged outside their doors, but inside this room, it was
deathly silent.

'We don't really even know each other,' she
said quietly, even as her heart was shifting, and
her mind was moving three steps ahead to her
inevitable acceptance.

Two main points were working on her to accept. Whatever threat he perceived, there was
enough of a basis in fact for Hannah to be seriously concerned. His wife and child had been
murdered. His father was in the mob. These
threats did not simply disappear—she was in
danger, and so was their daughter.

And even if it weren't for that, there were other
considerations. Hannah's parents had died un-
expectedly and her whole world had imploded.
She'd been moved to her aunt and uncle's—who
she'd barely known—and been left to their dubi-
ous care. She'd been miserable and alone.

There were no guarantees in life, but weren't
two parents better than one wherever possible?
Wasn't it more of an insurance policy for their
daughter to know both her mother and father?
What if Hannah insisted on raising her alone,
with Leonidas as a 'bit player' in their lives, and

then something happened to Hannah? And what if by then he'd married someone else, and their child was an outsider?

As Hannah had been.

She expelled a soft breath, the reality of that like a punch in the gut. Because marrying Leonidas would mean she'd always be on the edge, that she'd never find that one thing she knew she really wanted, deep down: a true family of her own. A family to which she belonged. People who adored and wanted her.

But this wasn't about her; it wasn't about her wants and desires. All that mattered was their baby.

With resignation in her turbulent green eyes, she lifted her head a little, partway to nodding.

He saw it, and his eyes narrowed then he straightened, relief in his features. 'We will fly to the island today. My lawyer will take care of the paperwork.'

But it was all so rushed. Hannah spun away from him, lifting her water bottle from the table's edge and sipping it.

'I have a job, Leonidas.'

'Quit.'

There were only two weeks left of her maternity contract. It wasn't the worst thing to do, though she hated the idea of leaving her boss in the lurch. She dropped her hand to her stomach and thought of their baby and nothing else seemed to matter.

For her? She'd do anything.

'You will be safe on the island,' he insisted, as though he could read her thoughts and knew exactly which buttons to press to get her to agree.

'On Chrysá Vráchia?' she asked distractedly.

'No.' His expression took on a contemplative look. 'My island.'

'You have your own island?' Disbelief filled the tone of her words.

'Yes. Not far from Chrysá.' He moved closer, his eyes scanning her face. 'It is beautiful. You'll like it.'

She was sure she would, but it was all happening so fast. Even knowing she would agree— that she had agreed—she heard herself say softly, 'This is crazy.'

And perhaps he thought she was going to change her mind, because he crossed the room and caught her arms, holding her close to him, his gaze locked to hers.

'You have to see that I cannot let our child be raised away from me. And, following that logic, that it is best for us to be married, to at least try to present our child with a sense of family, even when we know it to be a lie.'

Her heart squeezed tight, her lungs expelled air in a rush. Because it was exactly what she wanted, exactly what she'd just been thinking. Still, cynicism was quick to follow relief. 'You really think we can fool our child into believing we're a normal couple?'

His lips were a grim slash and she had the strongest impression that he couldn't have been less impressed if she'd suggested he set fire to this beautiful, enormous yacht.

'I think we owe it to our child to try.'

CHAPTER FIVE

HIS STATE-OF-THE-ART HELICOPTER flew them from the yacht to the airport, where his private jet was waiting.

It was the kind of plane Hannah had flown to Italy aboard, the kind that commercial airlines used, only it bore the name 'Leonidas Stathakis' in gold down the side. When she stepped on board it was exactly like walking into a plush hotel.

As with the yacht, everything was white or beige, and incredibly comfortable. Enormous seats, like armchairs, chandeliers made of crystal, and, deeper into the plane, a boardroom, a cinema and four bedrooms.

'Have a seat.' Leonidas indicated a bank of chairs, and as she did she couldn't shake the feeling that it was more like a job interview than anything else.

For the hundredth time since leaving his yacht, since lifting up into the sky and hovering over the picture-perfect Capri marina, Hannah questioned the wisdom of what she was doing.

But every time doubt reared its head and begged her to reconsider, she heard his words anew. *'My wife was murdered. As was my two-year-old son.'* And a frisson of terror sprinted down her spine and she knew she would do anything to avoid that same fate befalling their daughter.

Every primal, maternal instinct she possessed roared to life. She wouldn't allow their child to be harmed.

And nor would he.

She'd felt that promise from him and trusted him, had known he would lay down his own life if necessary to protect hers, to protect their child's.

And suddenly, the world seemed frightening and huge, and Hannah knew that if she walked away from Leonidas now, she would be alone, with unknown dangers lurking, with threats to their child she couldn't possibly appreciate, let alone avoid.

'The usual month-long notification period for weddings will be waived,' he explained, sitting opposite her, his long legs encroaching on her space so that if she wasn't very careful, they would be touching and the little fires still buzzing beneath her skin would arc into full-blown wildfires once more.

It took her a moment to collect her mind from the fears that were circulating and bring herself back to the present. 'Why?'

'What do you mean?'

Her sea-green eyes showed confusion. 'Well, isn't that the law? Why would that be changed for us?'

He lifted a brow and comprehension dawned.

'Because you asked for it to be, and you're Leonidas Stathakis.'

He shrugged. 'Yes.'

'And you get whatever you want?'

His eyes were like coal once more. 'No.'

Her heart twisted because of course he didn't. He'd just told her he'd lost his family—clearly his life wasn't that of a charmed man.

'Why rush, though, Leonidas?'

All of his attention was on her and she trembled for a different reason now, as the heat of his gaze touched something deep in her soul, stirring the remnants of their passion and desire anew. She swallowed, her throat dry, her cheeks blushing pink.

'Because there is no point in delay. Because I want you to be protected from this day, this moment. I will take no risks with our daughter's life,' he said firmly. 'Nor with yours. You should not have been brought into this.'

She opened her mouth to confront him, but he continued. 'Having sex with you was a moment of weakness, a stupid, selfish decision that I regretted instantly. Believe me, Hannah, if I could

take that back, if I could have never met you…'
He shook his head, looking away, as the plane
began to move on the runway.

'I am sorry to have drawn you into my world.
I am sorry that we must marry, sorry that we are
having a child together. It is my fault, all of it.
I cannot change that night, what happened between us, but I can do my damned best to ensure
no further harm befalls you.'

'Harm?' she repeated, the word just a croak.
'You think of this pregnancy as harm?'

'I think it is a mistake,' he muttered. 'But one
we must live with.'

Her temper spiked, disbelief at his callous
words making her chest hurt. 'How can you talk
about our baby like that?' she found herself whispering, even though that 'baby' was still very
much inside her.

'You said as much yourself,' he pointed out
logically. 'You didn't want this.'

'I didn't *plan* on it happening,' she corrected
caustically. 'I'm twenty-three years old; I thought
children would be way off in the future.'

He dipped his head in silent concession.

'But, Leonidas, almost as soon as I learned of
this pregnancy, I have loved this baby, and I have
wanted our daughter, and I have known I would
put this child first. For ever and always.'

He digested her words, his expression giving

little away, and then he nodded, as the plane hurtled faster down the runway before lifting into the sky.

'And in marrying me, I understand you are doing just that—putting our baby first. You do not wish for this marriage, and nor do I.' He ground his teeth together. 'And yet, for this child, here we are.' He reached into his pocket and pulled out his phone, not seeing the way her face paled at his harshly delivered words. 'I have some questions for you. My lawyer emailed them across.'

'Questions?' It was a rapid change of subject, one that made her head spin. 'What for?'

'The marriage licence. The prenuptial agreement. Setting up your bank accounts and the family trust.'

'Woah.' She was still reeling from his repeated insistence of how little he wanted this marriage, and, even though he was surely echoing her own thoughts, hearing them voiced made her head spin a little. It was all too much, too soon.

'Can't we just…take it one day at a time?'

'Let me make this clear,' he said, leaning forward, his expression that of a hard-nosed tycoon.

She swallowed, but refused to be cowed by his closeness, by his look of steel. 'Yes?'

'One week from today we will be married. You will be my wife: Mrs Hannah Stathakis. You will be marrying someone who is worth over a hundred billion American dollars. Your life, as you know it, is about to cease completely. There is no "taking it one day at a time". In what? Three months? Four? We will have a child. That is the deadline hanging over our heads. Within four months, we need to be able to find a way to relate, to exist as parents. We cannot delay. Surely you see that?'

It was all so shocking, so impossible to comprehend and also so reasonable. She heard his words and closed her eyes, because the final sentence was what really got through to her.

His net worth was awe-inspiring, his suggestion that she too might be worth a fortune, even his reminder that their daughter would inherit such a sum, were all details that caused her heart to pound, and not necessarily in a good way. But what he'd said that had really spoken to Hannah had been right at the end.

They had a deadline. A tiny little time bomb ticking away inside her belly.

They needed to find a way to make this work and he was showing himself to be cognisant of that.

'Your full name is Hannah May?'

'Hannah Grace May.' She nodded, tightening her seat belt and looking out of the window on autopilot. Capri was tiny beneath them, just a beau-

tiful picture-book piece of land, looming from
the sea, all verdant green against the deep blue
of the Med, the superyachts tiny white shapes
now, clean and crisp.

Was it really only that morning she'd flown
in over Italy, and stared down at this exact same
view? How certain she'd been then of being able
to tell Leonidas she was pregnant and then de-
part, confident he'd accept her suggestion of
being a small but vital part of their daughter's
life.

'Birth date?'

She responded, thinking back to her last birthday, right before Christmas. Angus had thrown
her a surprise dinner party and she'd pretended
to be thrilled, but Hannah hated surprises, and
she'd wondered how he couldn't know that about
her. She'd wondered how he could think she'd
like being the centre of attention like that, with
everyone in the restaurant staring at her, waiting
for her to smile and make a little speech thank-
ing them for coming.

Hannah didn't like surprises but she'd chalked
the party up to something they'd laugh about in
ten years' time. Besides, he'd gone to a huge
amount of effort, she wasn't about to be ungrate-
ful in the face of that.

She'd had no idea, though, that a way bigger
surprise had been in store for her, nor that his

'effort' in arranging such an elaborate party was undoubtedly his way of compensating for the fact he was sleeping with Hannah's cousin behind her back.

Her jaw tightened, and unconsciously she gripped her hands tightly in her lap, the past rushing towards her, wrapping around her, forcing her to look at it, to be in it even when it was strangling her. To remember the sight of her cousin and her fiancé, their limbs entwined, the dark black sheets of Angus's bed in stark contrast to their flesh, Michelle's white-blonde hair glistening in the evening light.

It was a betrayal on two fronts. That her fiancé would cheat on her was bad enough, but with someone she'd been raised to think of as a sister?

Indignation and hurt made her breath burn a little.

Capri swam beneath her, ancient and striking, and it offered a hint of perspective. How many millions of people had walked those shores, swum in these seas, each of them with their own problems and concerns, none of those concerns mattering, really, in the huge scheme of life and this earth? One day, she'd forget the sting of this betrayal, the second loss of family she'd had to endure.

'Parents' names?'

She swept her eyes shut, thinking of her biological parents, seeing her mother's smile as she tucked Hannah into bed, stroking her hair, singing their goodnight song.

'Ellie—Eleanor—and Brad.'

There were more questions and she answered them matter-of-factly—it was easier to simply provide the information than to launch into explanations with each point.

'Why did your engagement end?'

That question had her swivelling her head to him, and she was grateful that a flight attendant chose that exact moment to enter the cabin, offering drinks.

'Just water,' Hannah murmured.

'Coffee.' He focussed on Hannah. 'Are you hungry?'

She was. 'A little.'

'And some dinner.'

'Yes, sir.'

The attendant left, and Hannah thought—for a moment—Leonidas might have forgotten the question he'd posed. But of course he hadn't. This man probably never forgot a thing. 'Your fiancé?'

'Right.' She was surprised at how well she'd kept her voice neutral.

'He cheated on me.' She shrugged as though it didn't matter. 'It kind of killed my interest in marrying him.'

'I can imagine it would.' He was watching her

though she were simply a property he wanted to acquire, a piece of real estate he needed to buy.

Her own questions zipped through her. She sipped her water, balling her courage. 'Your wife and son…when did they…?'

His eyes were coal-like in his autocratic face. 'Almost five years ago.'

'I'm so sorry.' She spoke gently, softly. 'You said they were murdered?'

His eyes narrowed and his skin paled almost imperceptibly. 'Yes.'

'By whom?'

He held a hand up, silencing her with the gesture. 'I have no intention of discussing it, Hannah. My first marriage is off limits.'

The words smarted and she couldn't resist pointing out his hypocrisy. 'But you were just asking me about my fiancé.'

'You were happy to talk about it.'

Hannah's brow furrowed. 'No, I wasn't. I answered your questions because we're getting married.' How strange those words felt in her mouth. 'And if you're going to be my husband, it seems like the kind of thing you have a right to know about.'

He tilted his head in concession but his gaze was steady. 'I will not discuss Amy and Brax.'

Hannah expelled an angry rush of breath. 'Well, that seems kind of dumb.'

as though she were a puzzle he could put back together if only he had enough time. 'You hadn't slept with him. His idea, or yours?'

'His.'

His expression showed surprise. 'Why?'

The flight attendant reappeared with drinks, placing them down on the armrest table each had in their seat and leaving again.

'Romance.'

Leonidas lifted a brow. 'You think sex isn't romantic?'

Heat exploded through her body and she clamped her knees close together to stop them from shaking. Sex with Leonidas had gone beyond romance. It had been passion and fire, everything she could imagine wanting from a lover.

'I wouldn't know.' She dipped her eyes lower, studying the carpet on the floor of the aeroplane as though it were a fascinating work of art.

'So how come you were a virgin?' he pushed.

Hannah lifted her gaze, forcing herself to meet his curious eyes. 'We decided we'd wait.'

'There was no one before him?'

She bit down on her lip, shaking her head from side to side. 'Is that so unusual?'

His expression showed cynicism and disbelief. 'In my experience, yes.'

She laughed then, shaking her head a little. 'Stop looking at me like that.'

'Like what?'

'As though I'm some kind of… I don't know. As though I'm an alien.'

'Your inexperience is rare, that's all,' he corrected. 'Particularly given the fact you were engaged.'

'Angus and I…' She swallowed, the bitterness impossible to completely suppress. 'We were friends for a long time. The dating thing came out of nowhere and I guess our relationship didn't completely transition. Sex wasn't a drawcard for me. I guess it wasn't for him, either.'

'You did not desire him?'

Ridiculously, Hannah felt a buzz of disloyalty at admitting as much. 'Not really. We weren't about that.'

'What were you "about"?'

'I loved him,' she responded, simply, 'and I thought he loved me. That was enough.'

Leonidas nodded thoughtfully. 'So that was also a pragmatic marriage.'

Hannah's eyes widened at his description. 'What do you mean?'

'You agreed to marry a man simply because it made sense, because you thought you loved each other, without having any idea if you were physically compatible. So this marriage—ours—already has more going for it.'

Hearing him refer to their marriage caused her

heart to trip a little, banging against her sternum. 'How do you figure? Angus was one of my closest friends…'

'Which means very little given that he betrayed your trust and slept around behind your back.'

'Woah. Don't go easy on me, will you?'

'I don't think you want anyone to go easy on you, Hannah May.'

She startled a little at his unexpected perceptiveness. 'It was less than six months ago. It's still kind of raw.'

His expression barely shifted yet she had the feeling he was saving that little revelation, storing it away. 'He cheated on you. He doesn't deserve a second thought.'

She nodded, having said as much to herself.

'Is he still with her?'

Hannah reached for her water, sipping it, trying to tamp down on that little bundle of pain. 'No. Not according to my aunt.'

Leonidas nodded sharply, as if filing away that information. 'There is no love between you and me, Hannah, but there is desire enough to burn us alive if we are not careful. And there is a baby—which we both want to protect and cherish.'

'Yes. I do.'

'Neither of us wanted this, but we can make our marriage a success.' He said it with such fierce determination she almost laughed, as

He clearly hadn't been expecting that response. 'Oh, really?' There was danger in the silky drawl.

'Yeah, really.' The flight attendant returned, brandishing a platter loaded with Italian delicacies. Cheeses, ham, fruit, vegetable sticks and dips, breads, olive oil and vinegar. The aroma hit her in the gut and she realised she was actually starving.

But other feelings still took precedence. When they were alone again, she continued, 'You were married and had a son, and you lost them. You lost your family.'

Her voice caught because she knew more than enough about how that felt—to be safe in the bosom and security of your loved ones one day, then to be adrift at sea, cast out, alone, bereft, with none of the usual place markers to help you find your bearings.

'Thank you for the neat recitation of this fact.'

Her nostrils flared. 'I only mean that's a huge part of you. Don't you think our child will want to learn about her half-brother one day? That's a part of *her* life.'

Despite the fact his expression remained the same, his breath grew louder, and she would have sworn she saw panic cross his eyes.

'No.' He said the word like a curse, harsh and compelling.

Hannah sat perfectly still.

'She will never know about Brax. *Never.*'

Hannah's heart thumped hard in her chest.

'I will not speak of them. Not to you, not to her, not to anyone.'

She truly didn't think he meant it as an insult—he was caught on the back foot and the sheer strength of his emotions made him speak without thinking. But the vitriol in the statement sliced through her, filling her organs with acid.

'You're seeing this marriage, and our daughter, as an abstract concept,' she said gently, even when her heart was hurting. 'You're thinking of her as a baby only. What about when she's ten? Fifteen? Twenty? When you and she are friends as well as family, when she's sitting here where I am, on a plane, opposite you, and she's asking her father about his life. Do you really think you can keep such a huge part of yourself shielded from her? And me, for that matter?'

He drank his coffee, before piercing her with his jet-black eyes. 'Yes.'

'You're being incredibly obtuse and naïve.' But the words lacked zing. They were said with sympathy. No one knew more about the toll grief took when it was kept locked deep inside a person.

'I am sorry you think so.' He pushed his untouched plate aside and pulled a newspaper from the armrest. He flicked it up, pointedly blanking her.

It was galling, and only the fact that his stance was obviously driven by a deep, painful sadness kept her silent.

He didn't want to talk about his family. Yet.

They barely knew each other, despite this bizarre agreement they'd entered into. They would marry—in a week—and the very idea stirred her pulse to life. But despite the marriage, they'd spent only a few hours in one another's company. They were virtually strangers. Of course he didn't want to crack his heart open and lay everything out before her.

He was guarding his privacy, as befitted the newness of all this. Over time, as they grew to know one another, he was bound to change, to open up to her more.

She lifted a strawberry, popping it in her mouth, tasting the sweetness, relishing its freshness. She wanted him to trust her, and she had to show him how. To keep opening up to him, even when it felt counterintuitive, even when the past had shown her to be more guarded with herself, to protect her feelings.

'I felt undesirable,' Hannah murmured, reaching for another strawberry.

Leonidas pushed the top of the paper down, so his eyes could meet hers. There was a trace of coldness there, from their earlier conversation. She pushed on regardless.

'With Angus. I didn't really feel anything for him, physically, and he suggested we wait until we were married, so I agreed. I heard about couples not being able to keep their hands off each other and, honestly, I thought there was something wrong with me.'

She bit down on her lower lip thoughtfully. 'I presumed I just wasn't really sexual. I thought he wasn't, either. Then I saw him in bed with someone else, and I found out they'd been sleeping together for over a month, and the penny dropped. He was sexual. He liked sex. He just didn't want me.'

Leonidas placed the paper on his knees, his steady gaze trained on her face.

'I never felt like I wanted to rip a guy's clothes off. It was as though hormones left me completely behind.' She shrugged and then homed her own gaze in, focussing on his lips. Lips that were strong in his face, powerful and compelling. Lips that had kissed her and tipped her world upside down.

'But you…'

He arched a brow, silently prompting her to continue.

'You left me breathless,' she admitted, even when a part of her wondered if she should say as much, if it didn't leave her exposed and vulnerable, weakened in some way. 'I can't explain it. I felt desire for the first time in my life and I…'

'Go on,' he prompted, the words a little throaty, and she was so glad: glad that maybe he was affected by her confession in some way.

'I felt desirable for the first time in my life, too. I liked it. I liked the way you looked at me.' She turned away now, clearing her throat, looking towards the window.

Leonidas leaned forward, surprising her by placing his hand on hers. Sparks shot from her wrist and through her whole body. 'Your fiancé was an idiot for giving you a moment's doubt on this score.'

Her laugh was dismissive, but he leaned further forward, so their knees brushed. 'You are very, very sexy,' he said, simply, and heat began to burn in her veins.

'I don't mean that,' she said, shaking her head. 'You don't need to… I just meant to explain…'

'I know what you meant.' He sat back in his seat, regarding her once more. 'And I am telling you that you are a very sensual woman. You have no idea how I have been tormented by memories of that night, Hannah Grace May.'

CHAPTER SIX

THE MEDITERRANEAN GLISTENED just beyond the window of his study. On the second floor of his mansion, and jutting out a little from the rest of the building, this workspace boasted panoramic views of the ocean. Leonidas braced his arms on the windowsill, staring out at it, his breath burning in his lungs, his head spinning as comprehension sledged into him from both sides.

In Capri, he'd acted purely on instinct.

His wife and child had died, but here was another woman, another child, and they weren't Amy and Brax—they'd never be to him what Amy and Brax were—but they were still his responsibility.

The fact he would never have chosen to become a father again was a moot point.

She was pregnant.

They were having a child—a daughter.

His chest clutched and he slammed his eyes closed, the taste of adrenalin filling his mouth. A thousand and one memories tormented him from the inside out, like acid rushing through his veins.

Amy, finding out she was pregnant. Amy, swelling with his child. Amy, uncomfortable.

Amy, in labour. Amy, nursing their infant. Amy, watching Brax learn to walk. Amy, patiently reading to Brax, loving him, laughing at him.

Amy.

His eyes opened, bleakness in the depths of their obsidian centres.

If sleeping with another woman was a betrayal of Amy, what then was this? Creating a whole new family, and bringing them to this island?

He grunted, shaking his head, knowing that wasn't fair. Amy would never have expected him to close himself off from life, from another relationship, another family.

But Leonidas had sworn he would do exactly that.

The idea of Hannah ever becoming anything to him besides this was anathema. Theirs was a marriage born of necessity, a marriage born of a need to protect his child, and the woman he'd made pregnant. It was a marriage of duty, that was all.

Flint formed in his eyes, his resolution hardening.

They would marry—there was no other option. Even if it weren't for the possible threat to Hannah's life, Leonidas acknowledged his ancient sense of honour would have forced him to propose, to insist upon marriage. Growing up in the shipwreck of his father's marriages hadn't undone the lessons his grandfather had taught him, nor the unity he'd seen in his grandparents' marriage.

Their child, their daughter, deserved to grow up with that same example. Hannah deserved to have support and assistance.

And what else?

His body tightened as he flashed back to the way he'd responded to her that night, the way desire had engulfed him like a tidal wave, drowning him in his need for her. The way he'd kissed her, his mouth taking possession of hers, his whole body firing with a desperate need to possess her, even when he'd spent the past five months telling himself their night together had been a mistake.

It *had* been a mistake. It should never have happened, but it had, and, looking back, he didn't think he could have stopped it. Not for all the money in all the world. There had been a force pulling him to her; the moment their bodies had collided he'd felt as though he'd been jolted back to life. He'd looked at her and felt a surge of need that had gone beyond logic and sense. It had been an ancient, incessant beating of a drum and ignoring it had not been an option.

Perhaps it still wasn't…

Glass. Steel. Designer furniture. Servants. More glass. Famous art. Views of the ocean that just wouldn't quit. Hannah stared around Leonidas's mansion, the luxury of it almost impossible to grapple with, and wondered if she'd stepped into another dimension.

Did people really live like this?

He had his own airfield, for goodness' sake! His private jet had touched down on the island, a glistening ocean surrounding them as the sun dipped towards the horizon. She'd expected a limousine but there'd been several golf carts parked near the airstrip and he'd led her to one of them, opening the door for her in a way that made her impossibly aware of his breadth, strength and that musky, hyper-masculine fragrance of his.

When he'd sat beside her, their knees had brushed and she'd remembered what he'd said to her in the plane. *'You have no idea how I have been tormented by memories of that night.'*

Her belly stirred with anticipation and heat slicked between her legs.

At first, she hadn't seen the house. Mansion. She'd been too distracted by the beauty of this island. Rocky, primal in some way, just like Leonidas, with fruit groves to one side, grapevines running down towards the ocean and then, finally, a more formal, landscaped garden with huge olive and hibiscus trees providing large, dark patches of shade in the lead up to the house.

Leonidas had given her a brief tour, introducing Hannah to the housekeeper, Mrs Chrisohoidis, before excusing himself. 'I want to get some things organised.' He'd frowned, and she'd felt, for the first time, a hint of awkwardness at being here, in the house of a man she barely knew, whom she was destined to marry and raise a child with.

'Okay.' She'd smiled, to cover it, thinking that she had her own 'things' to organise. Like the room she was renting in Earl's Court and the job she was expected back at in a few days, and an aunt and uncle who deserved to know not only that she was pregnant but also that she was getting married.

None of these were obligations Hannah relished meeting and so she decided, instead, to explore. There was plenty of house to lose herself in, and with the approach of dusk, and only the occasional staff member to interrupt, she went from room to room, trying to get her bearings.

The property itself was spectacular. The initial impression that it was a virtual palace only grew as she saw more and more of it. But what she did realise, after almost an hour of wandering, was that there was a distinct lack of anything personal. Beyond the art, which must surely reflect something of Leonidas's taste, there was a complete lack of personal paraphernalia.

No pictures, no *stuff*. Nothing to show who lived here, nor the family he'd had and lost.

The sun finally kissed the sea and orange exploded across the sky, highlighted by dashes of pink. Hannah abandoned her tour, moving instead to the enormous terrace she'd seen when she'd first arrived. No sooner had she stepped onto it than the housekeeper appeared.

'Miss May, would you like anything to eat or drink?'

Hannah thought longingly of an ice-cold glass of wine and grimaced. 'A fruit juice?' she suggested.

'Very good. And a little snack?' The housekeeper was lined, her tanned skin marked with the lines of a life well-lived and filled with laughter. Her hair, once dark, had turned almost completely silver, except at her temples, where some inky colour stubbornly clung.

'I'm not very hungry.' Hannah wasn't sure why she said the words apologetically, only it felt a little as if the housekeeper was excited at the prospect of having someone else to feed.

'Ah, but you are eating for two, no?' And her eyes twinkled, crinkling at the corners with the force of her smile, and Hannah's chest squeezed because, for the first time since discovering her pregnancy, someone seemed completely overjoyed with the news.

Her flatmates had been shocked, her boss had been devastated at the possibility of losing someone he'd come to rely on so completely, and Leonidas had been…what? How had he felt? Hannah couldn't say with certainty, only it wasn't happiness. Shock. Fear. Worry. Guilt.

'My appetite hasn't really been affected,' she said.

'Ah, that will come,' the housekeeper murmured knowingly. 'May I?' She gestured to Hannah's stomach.

Mrs Chrisohoidis lifted her aged hands, with long, slender fingers and short nails, and pressed them to Hannah's belly and for a moment, out of nowhere, Hannah was hit with a sharp pang of regret—sadness that her own mother wouldn't get to enjoy this pregnancy with her.

'It's a girl?'

Hannah's expression showed surprise. 'Yes. How did you know?'

At this, Mrs Chrisohoidis laughed. 'A guess. I have a fifty per cent chance, no?'

Hannah laughed, too. 'Yes. Well, you guessed right.'

'A girl is good. Good for him.' She looked as though she wanted to say something more, but then shrugged. 'I bring you some bread.'

Hannah suppressed a smile and turned her attention back to the view, thinking once more of the beautiful coastline of Chrysá Vráchia, of how beautiful that island had been, how perfect everything about that night had seemed.

She'd longed to visit the island from the first time she'd seen footage of it in a movie and had been captivated by the cliffs that were cast of a stone that shimmered gold at sunrise and sunset. The fact she'd been able to book her flights so easily, the fact Leonidas had been there in the bar and she'd looked at him and felt an instant pull of attraction...the fact he'd reciprocated. It had all seemed preordained, right down to the conception of a child despite the fact they'd used protection.

When she heard the glass doors behind her slide open once more, she turned around with an easy smile on her face, expecting to see the housekeeper returning. Only it wasn't Mrs Chrisohoidis who emerged, carrying a champagne flute filled with orange juice.

'Leonidas.' Her smile faltered. Not because she wasn't happy to see him but because a simmering heat overtook any other thoughts and considerations.

'I am sorry I left you so long.'

'It's fine.' The last thing she wanted was for him to see her as an inconvenience—a house guest he had to care for. She knew the feeling well. Being foisted upon an unwilling aunt and uncle taught one to recognise those signs with ease. She ignored the prickle of disappointment and panic at finding herself in this situation, yet again.

This wasn't the same. She was an adult now, making her own decisions, choosing what was best for her child. 'You don't need to feel like you have to babysit me,' she said, a hint of defensiveness creeping into her statement.

His nod showed agreement with her words and, she thought, a little gratitude.

He didn't want to be saddled with a clinging housemate any more than she intended to be one.

'I will show you around, after dinner.'

'I've already had a look around,' she murmured, but her mind was zeroed in on his use of the word 'dinner'. It had all happened so fast she hadn't stopped to think about what their marriage would look like. Would it be this? Dinner together? Two people living in this huge house, pretending to be here by choice?

Or polite strangers, trapped in an elevator with one another, having to stay that way until the moment of escape? Except there was no escape here, no one coming to jimmy the doors open and cajole the lift into motion.

This was her life—his life.

'And I mean what I said. Please don't feel you

have to keep me company, or have dinner with me or anything. I know what this is.'

'*Ne?*' he prompted curiously.

Mrs Chrisohoidis appeared then, carrying not only some bread, but a whole platter, similar to the one they'd shared on the flight, but larger and more elaborate, furnished with many dips, vegetables, fish, cheeses and breads.

'I make your favourite for dinner.' She smiled at Leonidas as she placed the platter on a table towards the edge of the terrace.

'Thank you, Marina.'

They both watched her retreat and then Leonidas gestured towards the table.

'She's worked for you a while?' Hannah eyed the delicious platter as she sat down and found that, to her surprise, she was in fact hungry after all. She reached for an olive, lifting it to her lips, delighting in its fleshy orb and salty flavour.

'Marina?' He nodded. 'For as long as I can remember.'

That intrigued her. 'Since you were young?'

He nodded.

'So she worked for your parents?'

'Yes.'

A closed door. Just like his wife and son.

Hannah leaned against the balcony, her back to the view, her eyes intent on the man she was going to marry. 'Did you grow up here?'

He regarded her thoughtfully. 'No.'

'Where, then?'

'Everywhere.' A laconic shrug.

'I see. So this is also "off limits"?'

Her directness clearly surprised him. He smiled, a tight gesture, and shook his head. 'No. I simply do not talk about my parents often. Perhaps I've forgotten how.'

She could relate to that. Aunt Cathy had hated Hannah talking about her own mother and her father. *'He was my brother! How do you think it makes me feel to hear you going on about them? Heartbroken, that's how.'* And nine-year-old Hannah had learned to keep her parents alive in her own mind, her own head, rather than by sharing her memories with anyone else who could mirror them back to her.

Angus had asked about them, but by then she'd been so used to cosseting her memories that it hadn't come easily to explain what they'd been like.

'They divorced when I was young.'

'That was hard on you?'

'Yes.'

Mrs Chrisohoidis appeared once more, this time with a little bowl of chocolates. 'For the baby,' she said, and winked as she placed them down on the table.

'But there was a silver lining, too, because part of the divorce was a new brother.'

'How does that work?'

'My father had an affair. Thanos was the by-product. It caused my parents' divorce, but they'd been catastrophically miserable, anyway. I was glad they were separating; glad there would at last be some peace. And Thanos arrived, only three months my junior.'

'That must have been strange. How old were you?'

'Eight.'

'And he lived here?'

At this, Leonidas's expression was thoughtful, darkly so. 'His mother gave my father full custody.'

'That must have been hard for her.'

Leonidas shook his head. 'Hardest of all for Thanos, I'm sure.'

'How so?'

'His mother gave him up quite willingly,' Leonidas said softly, his expression shifting to one of compassion so Hannah's heart turned over in her chest. 'Thanos was—and remains—an incredibly strong-willed, stubborn character. She could not cope with him.'

Hannah's jaw dropped open. 'But he was just a boy! Surely there were ways of making him listen to her?'

'Who knows? But one day, when he was eight, she showed up and left him with my father. She said she couldn't do it any more.'

Sympathy scored deep in Hannah's veins. 'That must have been so hard for him. And your mother!'

'My mother hated him,' Leonidas said grimly. 'She treated him like a street dog.'

Hannah felt as though she could cry! Having experienced exactly this treatment herself, she felt an odd link to Leonidas's brother, a desire to look at him and comfort him, to tell him he was worthy, just as she'd always wished someone would say to her.

'But your father took him in,' Hannah said quietly, hoping there was a happy ending for the little boy Thanos had been.

'My father was bullish about custody. He had money, resources, staff. He ensured he had the raising of us. We were *his*, you see. Not boys so much as heirs. Proof of his virility. As I got older, I came to realise that he enjoyed the story of Thanos and my closeness in age. Far from finding it awkward, he relished the proof of his desirability. He boasted about it.'

Hannah ground her teeth together.

'You're not close to him?'

Leonidas took a sip of his wine; Hannah's gaze didn't falter. 'No.'

She had the feeling she was moving closer to ground he wished to remain private, topics he'd prefer not to discuss. Rather than approach it directly, she circled around it this time. 'Would you have preferred to stay with your mother?'

He frowned, thoughtfully. 'My mother was American. She moved to Las Vegas when they split. I didn't want to go.'

'It must have been hard for her. Leaving you, I mean.'

Leonidas's smile showed disagreement, but his response was a banal, 'Perhaps.'

'Do you see her much now?'

'Once a year, for an obligatory birthday visit.'

'Yours, or hers?'

'Hers.' He sipped his wine again, then turned to face Hannah. 'And you, Hannah?'

'What about me?'

His eyes swept over her face and then zeroed in on her lips, staying there for so long that they parted on a rushed breath and began to tingle; she was remembering his kiss and aching for it anew.

'What about your own parents?'

It was like being dragged into a well that was completely dark. She felt the blackness surround her and her expression closed off, her skin paling. She jerked her head, turning away from him and looking towards the horizon. The sun was gone but the sky remained tinged with colour.

Her breathing felt forced and unnatural and she struggled to find words.

'Hannah?'

She nodded. He had every right to ask—this street went both ways. She wanted to know about him, she had a strange, consuming curiosity to understand him. It made sense he would expect the same courtesy.

'My parents are dead.' How was it possible that those words still stung? It had been a long time; the reality of being orphaned was one she'd lived with for many years.

'I'm sorry.' She felt his proximity rather than saw him move closer. His body was behind hers, warm and strong, and instantly reassuring.

'It was years ago. I was only a child.'

He didn't say anything, but he was right there. If she spun around, they'd be touching.

'My mum used to love that movie—*The Secret Princess*. I watched it a little while after she'd died, and I wanted to go to Chrysá Vráchia ever since.'

He made a noise of comprehension and now she did turn, and, just as she'd expected, it brought their bodies together, his so strong and broad that she felt as if she could weather almost any storm if he was there.

'And then?' he prompted, shifting a little, so his legs were wider than her body, and he pressed his hands to the balcony balustrading behind her, so she was effectively trapped by him.

'Then?' Her voice was husky.

'You came to the island for New Year's Eve, to see the fireworks. What were you going to do then?'

'I hadn't really thought about it. But I guess in the back of my mind I always thought I'd end up in England. My mum was English so I have a passport and I've wanted to travel through Europe for ever.' Her expression was wistful. 'My honeymoon was going to be to Paris. I used to have a picture of the Eiffel Tower on my bedside table, and when you tapped a button on it the lights twinkled.' She shook her head wistfully. 'My parents gave it to me after a ballet recital and I've never been able to part with it.'

'You did ballet?'

'Only as a child,' she said, thinking of how her aunt had donated all Hannah's tutus and leotards to a community charity shop when Hannah had moved in. She pushed the memory aside, focussing on the present, on the circumstances that had brought her here. 'After I found Angus and Michelle in bed together, I just wanted to run away.'

'Naturally.'

'It seemed as good a time as any to pack up and see the world.' Her smile was wry. 'I left before I could change my mind.'

Leonidas nodded thoughtfully. 'Have you spoken to him since you left?'

'No. There's nothing more to say there.'

'You were friends before you became engaged?'

'Yes.'

'You don't miss his friendship?'

Hannah thought of Michelle and Angus and her life in Australia and dropped her gaze. 'I miss a lot of things. It's hard, having the rug pulled out from under you.' She lifted her eyes to his, sympathy softening her features as she remembered his own harrowing past. 'As you would know.'

A warning light glinted in his eyes. *Don't go there.*

'Who was the other woman?' His voice was gruff.

Hannah's heart constricted with now familiar pain. 'That was the really hard part.'

'Harder than your fiancé cheating on you?'

'Yeah.' She angled her face, so Leonidas had a perfect view of her profile, delicate and ethereal.

'Who was she?' he repeated, and Hannah sucked in a soft breath.

'My cousin, Michelle. More like a sister, really. After Mum and Dad died, I went to live with my aunt and uncle, and Michelle.'

He let out a soft whistle. *'Christós.'*

'Yeah.' Her laugh was a low rumble. 'You

could say that, and I did—worse, in fact. I was devastated.'

Admitting that felt good. Saying the word aloud, Hannah recognised that she hadn't spoken to another soul about the affair.

'I lost everything that afternoon.'

'What did your aunt and uncle say?'

Hannah lifted her gaze to his, and a ridiculous sense of shame made it difficult to maintain eye contact. Hannah shook her head, that awful afternoon burned into her brain like a cattle brand. 'Do you mind if we don't go down this particular memory lane?'

She flicked her gaze back to his face, catching surprise crossing his features. But it was banked down within a moment, and he stepped back, almost as though he hadn't realised how close they were, how he was touching her.

'Of course.' His smile didn't reach his eyes. 'Have a seat.' He gestured towards the table. 'There is much we have to discuss.'

CHAPTER SEVEN

'What work were you doing in London?'

Hannah sipped her fruit juice, a pang of guilt scrunching her chest when she thought of her boss, Fergus, and how she planned to leave him completely in the lurch.

'I'm a legal secretary.'

'Have you done this for long?'

She nodded thoughtfully. 'Since I left high school. My aunt and uncle lived in a small town. There weren't a lot of options for work. I would have loved to go away to university but it just wasn't practical.'

'For what reason?'

'Money, mainly.'

'I thought universities in Australia were subsidised?'

'They are,' she agreed, lifting a piece of fish from the platter. 'But I'd have had to move to the city, found a place to rent. Even with governmental assistance, I wouldn't have been able to afford to live out of home, to cover textbooks and rent.'

'Your parents left you nothing when they died?'

She felt censure in his voice and her back

straightened, defensiveness stirring inside her. 'They left a little. My aunt and uncle took a stipend each year, and what's left I can't claim until I'm twenty-five.'

At this, Leonidas was completely still. 'Your aunt and uncle took money from you?'

'It wasn't like that,' she said quietly. 'They took money to cover the cost of raising me.'

His face showed pure contempt.

'You think that was wrong?'

A muscle jerked in his jaw and she felt he was weighing his words, choosing what to say with care. She didn't know him well and yet she felt for herself how uncharacteristic that care was.

'I do,' he said finally. 'Were they struggling financially?'

Hannah shifted her shoulders and repeated the line she'd frequently been given. 'An extra person is an extra expense.'

He studied her thoughtfully for several seconds, but he evidently decided not to pursue this line of questioning, and she was glad.

Glad because she didn't like to talk about it, much less think about it.

As a teenager, she'd been able to ignore her niggling doubts, but as she'd grown older, and met more people, she had come to see more and more at fault with the way her aunt and uncle had treated her. A desire to defend them didn't change reality, and the reality felt an awful lot as if they simply resented her presence in their lives.

She felt it in her heart, but to confess that to Leonidas was too difficult.

'What would you have studied?'

She relaxed visibly. 'That's easy.'

He waited, his eyes not shifting from her face, so that even when their conversation was smoother to navigate, her pulse was still racing.

He had beautiful eyes, but she doubted many women told him that. There were too many other things about him that required mention. His body, his lips, his clever, clever hands. But his eyes were breathtaking. Dark, rimmed with thick black lashes, and when the full force of their focus was given to one's face, concentration was almost impossible.

'Am I to guess?' he prompted, after several seconds.

Heat flooded her cheeks. 'I wanted to be a lawyer,' she said, curling her fingers around the stem of her orange juice–filled champagne flute, feeling its fine crystal. 'Law degrees take years and cost a bomb. The textbooks alone would have bankrupted my aunt and uncle.' She said it with a smile, as though it were a joke. 'Becoming a legal secretary was the next best thing. There was a conveyancing firm in another town, just a half-hour drive away. Angus worked there.' She cleared her throat, sipping her drink. 'That's how we met.'

'I see.' If it were possible, his expression darkened even further.

'I loved working at the firm, and I'm good at what I do.' Pride touched her voice. 'So maybe everything worked out for the best.'

'I can't say I agree with that,' he drawled, after several long moments. His eyes roamed her face. 'However, you no longer have any kind of financial impediment to you undertaking a law degree. You will obviously be based here, on the island, but there are many universities that offer degrees via distance. You could enrol in one to start next semester.'

Hannah's eyes were huge, and she was struck dumb, for many reasons.

'This island is beautiful,' she said thoughtfully, trying to imagine her future. 'But very remote.'

His expression glittered. 'Yes. By design.'

She nodded, the loss of his family naturally having made him security conscious. Nonetheless, the idea of being stuck here sat strangely in her chest. She liked a tropical paradise as much as the next person, but not without an easy escape route.

Not necessarily for ever. She shelved her thoughts, though. They'd only just arrived. There was time to find her groove as they adjusted to this new life.

'I love the idea of studying law as much as ever,' she said sincerely. 'But I'm kind of going to have my hands full for the next little while…'

'A baby is not an excuse to turn your back on your dreams,' he said simply. 'You will want for nothing, and help will be available whenever you need it. I will be available,' he added. 'This is *our* daughter, not your burden alone.'

Her heart turned over in her chest and his completely unexpected show of support and confidence had her opening a little of herself up to him.

'I'm nervous, Leonidas.' She lifted the fish to her mouth, chewing on it while she pulled her thoughts into order. 'The idea of becoming a mum scares me half to death.'

'Why?'

'How can it not? I have no idea what to do, or if I'll be any good at it. I mean, it's a *baby*. I've never even had a pet.'

His laugh was just a dry, throaty husk of a sound. 'A baby is not really anything like a pet, so I wouldn't let that bother you too much.'

'You know what I mean. I've never had the responsibility of keeping something alive, something totally dependent on me.'

She heard the words a second too late, before

she could catch them, but as soon as they landed in the atmosphere she wished she could gobble them right back up. 'I'm sorry.' She leaned across the table and put a hand on his, sympathy softening her expression while his own features tightened to the point of breaking.

'Don't be. I know what you meant.'

She nodded, but the easy air of conversation had dissipated.

'Being nervous is normal. You just have to trust that you will know what to do when our baby is born.'

'And you have experience,' she said, watching him carefully.

'Yes.' He nodded, curtly, placing his napkin on his side plate and sipping his wine. Then, he stood, fixing her with a level stare. 'Marina will show you to your room when you are finished. In the morning, a stylist will arrive to take your clothes order, and then a jeweller will come to offer you some rings to choose from.'

She blinked up at him, his abrupt change of temperament giving her whiplash. He was obviously hesitant to discuss his first wife and son, but jeez!

'Leonidas…' Hannah frowned, not sure what she wanted to say, knowing only that she didn't want him to walk away from her like this. 'I can't ignore the fact you had a family before this. I get that you don't like talking about it, but I can't tiptoe around it for ever. You had a son, and I'm pregnant with your daughter. Don't you think it's natural that we'll talk about him, from time to time?'

'No.' He thrust his hands into his pockets and looked out to sea, the expression on his face so completely heartbroken that something inside Hannah iced over, because it was clear to her, in that moment, how hung up he still was on the family he'd lost.

And why wouldn't he be? They'd been wrenched from him by a cruel twist of fate, by the acts of a madman. Nothing about this—his situation—was by his choice.

Nor was it Hannah's, she reminded herself. She knew more than her fair share about cruel twists of fate.

The sky was darkening with every second, but pinpricks of light danced obstinately through, sparkling like diamonds against black sand. She followed his gaze, her own appetite disappearing.

'I don't want to force you,' she said gently, standing to move right in front of him. 'It's your grief, and your life. But I will say, as someone who's spent a very long time bottling things up, that it's not healthy.' She lifted a hand, touching the side of his cheek. He flinched, his eyes jerking to hers, showing animosity and frustration.

Showing the depths of his brokenness.

It called to Hannah; she understood it.

'You are an expert in grief, then?' he pushed, anger in the words.

'Sadly, yes,' she agreed quietly.

'Do not compare what we have experienced,' he said. 'To lose your parents is unbearable, I understand that, and I am sorry for you, what you went through. You were a child, robbed of the ability to be a child. But I caused my wife and son's death. As sure as if I had murdered them myself, I am the reason they died. Do not presume to have any idea what that knowledge feels like.'

That Hannah slept fitfully was hardly surprising. Leonidas's parting shot ran around and around her mind, the torment of his admission ripping her heart into pieces. To live with that guilt would have driven a lesser man crazy.

But it wasn't only sadness for the man she'd hastily agreed to marry.

It was worry.

Fear.

Panic.

Stress.

And something far, far more perplexing, something that made her nipples pucker against the shirt he'd given her to sleep in, that made her arch her back in her dreams, and meant she felt warm and wet between her legs when she finally gave up on trying to sleep, before dawn, and stood, pacing to the window that overlooked the ocean.

Memories.

Memories of their one night together and fantasies of future nights were all weaving through Hannah's being, bursting upon her soul and demanding attention.

The sun had just started to spread warmth over the beach. Darkness was reluctantly giving way to light, and the morning was fresh.

It was Hannah's favourite time of day, when the air itself seemed to be full of magic and promise.

She had only the clothes she'd worn the day before, and the shirt she'd slept in, which was ridiculously big even when accommodating her pregnant belly. Still, it was comfortable and covered her body. Besides, it was a private island. Who was going to see her?

Pausing only to take a quick drink of water in the kitchen, Hannah unlocked the front door of the mansion and stepped out, breathing in the tangy salt air.

Excitement and a sense of anticipation rushed her out of nowhere, like when she was a small girl, around six or seven, and her parents had taken her away on their first family vacation.

They'd gone to the glitzy beachside resort of Noosa, in tropical Queensland, and Hannah had woken early and looked out on the rolling waves crashing onto the beach, the moon still shimmering in the sky, and her stomach had rolled, just like this.

There's something elemental and enlivening about the sea, and this island was surrounded by a particularly pristine shoreline and ocean.

Without having any real intention of going to the beach, she found herself moving that way quickly, her bare feet grateful when they connected with cool, fine sand, clumps of long grass spiking up between it every now and again. Dunes gave way to the flatness of the shore. She walked all the way to the water's edge, standing flat-footed and staring out to the sea, her back to Leonidas's mansion, her eyes on the horizon.

This was not the tropical water off the coast of Queensland. Here, there were no waves, only the gentle sighing of the sea as the tide receded. With each little pause, each undulation back towards the shore, the water danced over Hannah's toes; the cool was delicious given the promise of the day's heat.

She could have stood there, staring out at the mesmerising water, all day, were it not for the sudden and loud thumping from directly to her left. She turned just in time to see Leonidas, earphones in and head down, eyes trained on the shore, galumphing towards her. There was barely enough time to sidestep out of his way.

He startled as he ran past, jerking his head up at the intrusion he'd sensed, then swore, pulling his earphones out and letting them dangle loose around his neck.

She wished he hadn't.

The simple act drew her eyes from his face to his body. There was nothing scandalous about what he was wearing. Shorts and a T-shirt—only the T-shirt was wet with perspiration and the firmness of his pecs was clearly visible.

She took a step backwards without realising it, not to put physical space between them but because she wanted to see him better. Her aunt would have told her to stop staring, but Hannah couldn't. As much as the tide couldn't cease its rhythmic motion, Hannah found it impossible to tear her eyes away.

She remembered everything about him and yet…seeing him again sparked a whole new range of wants and needs.

Thick, strong legs covered in dark, wiry hair looked capable of running marathons but she couldn't look at him without imagining him straddling her, pushing her to the sand and bringing his body over hers, his hard arousal insistent between her legs. Without remembering the feeling of his weight on her body, his strength, power and skill in driving her to orgasm again and again.

Her throat was dry and the humming of the ocean was nothing to the furious pounding of her own blood in her ears.

She dragged her eyes up his body, over dark shorts that showed nothing of his manhood, even when she was suddenly desperate to see it—to see all of him again, in real life, not her very vivid dreams.

She prepared to meet his gaze, knowing he must surely be regarding her with mocking cynicism, only he wasn't.

He wasn't looking at her face, wasn't looking at her eyes to see the way she'd been eating him alive. No, he was performing his own slow, sensual inspection and it was enough to make her blood burn.

His eyes were on her legs, desire burning in the depths of his gaze as he lifted his attention to the curve of her breasts and, finally, to her lips. They parted under his inspection as she silently willed him to kiss them. To pull her into his arms and remember how well that worked between them.

And when he didn't, she took a step forward herself, knowing it didn't matter who moved first, knowing it was imperative only that they touch once more.

It broke the spell. His gaze slammed into hers, surprise there, confusion and, yes, desire. So much desire that it almost drowned her. He made a deep, husky sound and stood completely still, his body hard like steel.

Hannah moved closer, her eyes holding a silent challenge. *Stop me if you dare.*

He didn't.

One more step and their bodies connected, just like that first night in the bar, when fate had thrown them together and passion had held them there.

The air around them cracked and sizzled as though a localised electrical storm had touched down. He was so much bigger than she was. Hannah stood on the tips of her toes, which brought her body flush to his, her womanhood so close to the strength of his arousal that she echoed his own guttural moan with a soft whimper.

'Hannah.' Her name on his lips wasn't a request, nor was it a surrender. He spoke her name as though he simply couldn't resist and she lifted higher onto her toes and kissed him, hungrily.

He was still. Completely still, so her mouth moved over his, her tongue tracing the outline of his lower lip, her breath warm against him, and then, after the briefest moment, he lifted his hands to the back of her head, holding her where she was, keeping her so close to him, and he opened his mouth, kissing her back. But not in the way she had kissed him.

This was a kiss driven as much by a need to possess as his kiss had been the first night they'd met. There was madness in his kiss, his desperation for her completely overwhelming.

The water rushed around them, chasing their ankles, its fervent pursuit matched by the coursing of blood in their veins.

Hannah couldn't have said if he pulled her to the sand or if she pulled him, but she was lying down then, her back against the cold ground, her legs bent, Leonidas's body on hers, just as she'd fantasised about, his weight sheer bliss.

His kiss didn't relent, even as his hands pushed her shirt up, revealing the scrap of her underwear.

He disposed of them and then his own shorts, lifting himself up to look at her, his eyes piercing her, confusion and something else moving through him.

'I told myself we wouldn't do this,' he groaned, his voice tormented.

She bit down on her lower lip, her own heart tripping in her chest as his arousal nudged at her sex.

'Why not?'

His answer was to nudge his arousal inside her, and she moaned low in her throat as she felt the power of his possession. It had been five months but her body welcomed him back as though he were her saviour. She arched her back instinctively, needing more, and he drove himself deeper, pushed up on his elbows so he could see her, watch her, as well as feel her reactions.

Her insides squeezed him tight, muscles convulsing around him as he stretched her body to accommodate his length.

'What are you doing to me?' he groaned, and then said something in his native tongue, the words, spiced and warm, flickering inside her blood.

'I don't know but you're doing it right back,' she whispered, digging her nails into his shoulders before running them lower, finding the edge of his shirt and lifting it, trailing her fingertips over his back, feeling his smooth, warm skin beneath her and revelling in the contact.

Higher the shirt went, until he pushed up off one arm, ripping it from his body and casting it aside, so that he was naked on top of her. She wanted to stare at him, but she was incapable of forming the words to demand that when he was moving inside her, his body calling to hers, demanding her response, invoking ancient, soul-deep rhythms and needs.

'*Christós...*' The word was dark, a curse and a plea. His expression was taut as he looked down at her, unable to fathom her, this, them. 'Who are you?'

There was no answer she could give; the question made little sense.

He didn't require an answer, in any event. He moved faster then, his hands cupping her breasts, his mouth possessing hers as he kissed her until she saw stars and his hard arousal thrust deep inside her and everything she was in the past and would be in the future seemed to be coalescing in that one single, fragile moment.

She dug her nails into the curve of his buttock as pleasure pounded against her, like one of those waves from her faraway childhood, incessant, demanding, ancient. She cried his name and he stilled, his body heavy on hers, but as she exploded with pleasure her muscles squeezed him tight and Leonidas dropped his arms to his side, holding himself steady above her, staring down at her, watching every last second of delirium take over her body.

He stared at her so that when she blinked her eyes open, her own disorientation at what had just happened filling her with uncertainty, he saw it and he dropped his head, kissing her again, as though he knew how much she needed it.

It was a brief reprieve, nothing more. She'd been drowned by their passion and then emerged for air, and now Leonidas was taking her back under with him, tangling her in his limbs, his hands roaming all of her body now, until he curved them behind her bottom and lifted her a little off the sand, so his arousal reached even deeper and she found insanity was once more in pursuit.

His name tripped off her tongue, pushing into his mouth. With every thrust of his arousal, his body tightened, his buttocks squeezing, his muscles firm. She felt him beneath her palms, all of him, and then he moved faster, deeper and she was lifting into the heavens again, her body weightless and powerless to resist.

He moved inside her and she called his name as she burst apart at the seams, *Leonidas*, over and over. She called to him—willing him to answer—and he did. He tangled his fingers through hers, lifting Hannah's arms up above her head, his eyes on hers intense as his own explosion wracked his body, his release simultaneous with hers.

Their breath was frantic, louder than the ocean and the flapping of birds overhead, their exhalations thick and raspy, drenched in urgency. Pleasure had made her lungs expire. He lay on top of her and she ran her fingers down his back, still mesmerised by the feeling of his skin, and this: the closeness, the weight, the intimacy.

It lasted only seconds, and then Leonidas was

rolling off, beside Hannah, onto his back on the sand beside her, staring at the dawn sky.

'*Christós...*' He said the word low and thick. 'What are you?'

Again, a question that was almost impossible to answer. He turned his head to stare at her and there was confusion in his eyes, and a look of resignation.

'What do you mean?'

He reached out as though he couldn't help himself, his fingers catching a thick section of her hair and running through it, his eyes on the brassy tones.

'Are you real?'

The question made no sense.

She raised an eyebrow, propping up on one elbow, a smile tugging at her lips. 'I'm pretty sure I am.'

He didn't smile. 'I swore we wouldn't do this.'

Hannah expelled a sigh. 'You said that. I heard you. It doesn't make sense, though.'

His frown deepened. 'For four years I have been able to resist any woman in the world. For four years I have been single, and then you...'

Hannah was quiet as his words ran through her mind and their meaning became clear. 'You mean you hadn't been with anyone since Amy died?'

His expression was shuttered. He shook his head, his lips a grim line in his face. 'No.'

Hannah's chest hurt, as if it had been sliced in half and cut wide open. 'Why not?'

His nostrils flared. 'Many reasons.' His hand lifted to her hair again, toying with the ends. 'I enjoyed resisting temptation, choosing to be celibate, to be alone. And then I saw you and it was just like this. As though you are some kind of angel—or devil—sent to tempt me even when I know how wrong this is. I spent four years flexing my power here and you take it away from me completely.'

Hannah's voice was thick; she didn't know if she was flattered or insulted. She suspected a bit of both. 'Why is it wrong?'

He pushed up to standing then, just as he had the night before when she'd touched on areas he preferred not to discuss.

But she wasn't going to let him get away with it twice. 'I'm serious, Leonidas. *Why* is this wrong?'

CHAPTER EIGHT

SHE WAITED AND WAITED and after a moment, she wondered if he wasn't going to answer her. He simply stood there, naked as the day he was born, staring out to sea, and she moved towards him, coming around in front of him so she could look up into his stubborn face.

'I don't know much about sex,' she said slowly, when he remained silent. 'But I do know that I want to feel more of this.' She gestured from him to her. 'I do know this is amazing and hot and incredibly addictive.'

He ground his teeth together, the action making his jaw tight, his expression grim. 'That night shouldn't have happened.'

Hannah shook her head, rejecting both the words and the sentiment. 'Neither of us planned that it would, just like we didn't plan for this to happen, but that doesn't mean it was wrong.'

He looked at her then, his expression impossible to interpret. 'You are so young.'

He said it as though it were a criticism.

'I'm twenty-three.'

'Yes, but you've been very sheltered.' He cupped her face then. 'You deserve better than this.'

'Than marriage to you?'

'Better than a lifetime with me.' His lips were grim. 'I'm not the man you want me to be.'

'And what do I want you to be?'

He expelled a soft breath then stepped back a little, just enough to put some distance between them. 'A clean slate.'

The words were strange. Discordant. At first, she couldn't make sense of them. But as he turned and pulled his shorts on, she saw the weight on his shoulders, the ghosts that chased him, and comprehension shifted through her.

'You're wrong.' She dropped the words like little, tiny bombs. He didn't turn around, but he froze completely still, so she knew he was listening. 'I know you have a past, just like I do. But I'm not going to marry you if you're telling me I'm going to be living with a brick wall. I'm not getting married if I think there's no hope of having a living, breathing, red-blooded man as my husband.'

He turned around then, his expression bleak at first, and then filling with frustration. 'And sex ticks that box for you?'

Hannah frowned. That hadn't been what she'd meant, but at the same time she knew it was a start. What they shared, physically, was a true form of intimacy. She didn't need to have loads of experience to recognise that. She could see it in his eyes when he held her. She could feel the uniqueness of what they shared. He was trying to fight it, and she knew why.

Intimacy like this must surely lead to more.

With Angus, she'd operated on the reverse assumption. She'd hoped their friendship would bridge the way to a satisfying physical relationship. And it might have, but it would never have been like this.

Nothing like it.

This kind of connection couldn't be learned.

It was raw and organic, primal, between two people.

She glared at him, challenging him from the depths of her soul. 'Yes,' she agreed. 'I'm not going to live here like a prisoner in a gilded cage, Leonidas.' Her voice cracked as she firmed up on that resolution. 'This island is stunning but it's no place to live if you're going to freeze me out.'

'Does it look like I am freezing you out?'

'But you want to,' she insisted. 'You want to fight this, not build on it.'

His features tensed, his lips just a gash in his face, and she knew she was right.

'And I won't stay here if that's the case.' She tilted her chin bravely, when outside this island was a world she wasn't sure she trusted any more. The reality of his wife and son's murder was still exploding inside her, and she didn't doubt there could be a risk to her.

But there was risk here, too. Risk in living with a man who was determined to ice her out. What if he acted the same with their daughter? What if she were born and Leonidas made no effort to get to know her?

His eyes narrowed. 'How? You forget my island is practically inaccessible to anyone but me...'

Hannah was breathless again, her pulse racing but for a wholly different reason. 'Are you seriously threatening to kidnap me?'

Frustration zipped through his body. 'No.' He raked a hand through his hair. '*Christós*, Hannah. You can't leave the island.'

'Ever?' she demanded, crossing her arms over her chest to still the frantic hammering of her heart.

'Not on your own,' he amended. 'I was careless once before, I cannot risk it again. I won't have more on my conscience.'

And her rapidly thumping heart softened, aching, breaking for Leonidas.

'I'm so sorry you lost them,' she said quietly. 'But I'm not going to be a prisoner to your fears.'

'They should be your fears, too.'

'I want to keep our daughter safe.' Her voice was level, careful. 'Somewhere between me living out there on my own and the luxurious prison you're proposing is a middle ground we need to find.'

His eyes held hers for several beats. 'I cannot agree to that.' The words were wrenched from him, gravelled and thick with emotion.

'Why not?' she demanded, her hands shifting to her hips.

'You cannot imagine what it was like,' he said, grimly. 'To get that call, to see their bodies.' He shook his head from side to side and stopped speaking, but his face was lined with grief.

Tears bit at the back of Hannah's throat; sympathy rushed through her. 'I can't even imagine that, you're right.' She lifted a hand to his chest, running it over his muscled flesh.

'I made a choice after they died. I planned to stay single for the rest of my life.'

Hannah's stomach clenched.

'I didn't want this. I have done everything I could to avoid it.' His words were heavy with despair. She felt it and wished she could take it away, but how? 'I knew we shouldn't have slept together. It was so selfish of me but I was careful, Hannah. I did everything I could to make sure this wouldn't happen. I didn't want this.'

She wasn't sure when she'd let herself care enough about him that his words would hold such a latent power to wound, but they cut her deep.

'You shouldn't have to live in this—what did you call it? Gilded prison? Because of me.'

She couldn't speak.

'But you do.' The words were grim. 'Surely you can see that? I can't risk anything happening to you, to her.' He lifted a hand to Hannah's stomach, curving it over the bump there. His eyes met Hannah's with a burning intensity.

'Let me protect you both. Please.'

'I am,' she said, quietly, stroking his chest, her eyes determined. 'But this is my life we're talking about.'

He gazed at her, his expression strangely uncertain. 'I know that.'

'I want to marry you.' The words felt right, completely perfect. 'I know it's the sensible decision.' And strength surged inside her. 'When my mum and dad died, I lost everything. Our home, my community, my school, my friends. I went to live somewhere new and different and I was miserable,' she said, frankly, so captivated by her past that she didn't see the way his expression changed with the force of his concentration.

'I don't want our daughter to ever know that kind of uncertainty. You're her dad, and by doing this together, she'll have two people who can love her and look after her. And as she grows older, we'll surround her with other people who'll love her and know her, so that if anything *ever* happened to us and she were left alone, she would eventually be okay. Don't you see that, Leonidas? I need her to be okay, just like you do, but, for me, one of the worst things we can do is isolate her. Keep her locked up from this world, so we're the only people she ever really knows. She deserves to live a full and normal life.'

'How come you were sent to live with your aunt and uncle?'

Hannah frowned. 'There wasn't anyone else.'

'And you didn't know them well?'

'No.' She shook her head. 'I'd only met them a few times. They weren't close to my parents.'

He frowned, lifting his hands to her face and cupping her cheeks. He stared down at her, his eyes ravaging her face. 'You were deeply unhappy there?'

Hannah didn't want to think of her life in those terms; she hated feeling like a victim. And yet, what could she say? She'd been miserable. Only now that she was on the other side of the world and free from her aunt's catty remarks did she realise what an oppressive weight they'd been on her shoulders.

'I wasn't happy.' She softened the sentiment a little. 'I'm not sure my aunt ever really liked me, let alone loved me.'

He scanned her face but said nothing.

'I spent more than a decade living with people who cared for me out of a sense of obligation. People who resented my presence, who undoubtedly wished I wasn't in their life. I won't do it again.' Her eyes showed determination. 'We didn't plan this, we didn't intend for it to happen, but that doesn't mean we can't make this marriage work.'

Still, he was silent.

'Less than six months ago, I was engaged to another man. I had my whole life planned out, and it looked nothing like this. I'm not an idiot, Leonidas. If I ever believed in fairy tales, I've learned my lesson many times over. This isn't a perfect situation, but there's enough here to work with. Our marriage can be more than a business arrangement, a deal for shared custody. We can make something of this—we just have to be brave enough to try.'

His jaw was square as he turned to the water, looking at it, his face giving little away. 'I want you to be safe and, yes, I want you to be happy, Hannah. I want our daughter to have the best life she can. But beyond that, stop expecting things of me. You say you no longer believe in fairy tales? Then do not turn me into any kind of Prince Charming in your mind. We are a one-night stand we can't escape, that's all.'

CHAPTER NINE

HANNAH STARED AT the black velvet box with a sense of disbelief. The jeweller was watching her, a smile on his face, and Hannah imagined how this must look from the outside. A tailor had arrived on the island earlier that day, armed with suitcases of couture, beautiful dresses, jeans, shirts, bathers, lingerie—everything the wife of Leonidas Stathakis might be expected to wear.

The dressmaker had stayed for hours, taking Hannah's measurements, and photographs of her for 'colour matching'—whatever that was—and to discuss wedding dress options, before disappearing again. All the while some servant or other had taken the suitcases and carefully unpacked them into the room Hannah was using.

'Her room,' though she had no idea when she'd ever think of it like that.

There had also been a doctor, who'd come to check her over and implement a new vitamin regimen, and promised fortnightly check-ups. Then there'd been a more detailed conference with Mrs Chrisohoidis regarding Hannah's favourite foods, flowers and any other thoughts she might have as regards the running of the house.

Hannah had changed into one of the simple white shift dresses—for comfort on a hot day—and pulled her red hair into a bun on top of her head. As she looked at the dozen engagement rings the jeweller presented, all set against signature turquoise velvet, she knew it must appear to be some kind of Cinderella fairy tale. Leonidas looked on, not exactly playing the part of Prince Charming, though what he lacked in warmth he more than made up for in physical appeal.

He was casually dressed, in shorts and a white shirt, but that did nothing to diminish his charisma and the sense of raw power that emanated from his pores. It burst into the room, making it almost impossible for Hannah to keep her mind focussed on this task.

'Just something simple,' she said with a shake of her head, thinking that each and every ring was way too sparkly and way, way too big. 'Maybe this one?' She chose the smallest in the box.

'Ah!' The jeweller nodded. 'It is very beautiful.' He lifted it out, holding it towards Hannah. 'Try it on.'

This was all wrong! She didn't want to choose her own engagement ring, and no matter how many pretty, sparkly, *enormous* diamonds twinkled at her, it didn't feel right. She closed her eyes for a moment and imagined Leonidas going down on one knee, proposing as though this were a real wedding, and a bolt of panic surged inside her. But this wasn't a fairy tale and he wasn't Prince Charming, just as he'd said.

We are a one-night stand we can't escape.

Her heart began to churn. With a sense of unease, as though she were about to commit massive tax fraud, she slid the ring onto her finger. It was a perfect fit. She stared down at it and, ridiculously, tears filled her eyes. Now! Here! After becoming so adept at blocking them, she felt their salty promise and quickly sought to disguise them in what should have been a happy moment.

'It's beautiful.'

Leonidas came to stand beside her, his presence a force, a magnetic energy, pulling her eyes upwards.

'Don't you think?' she asked him.

His eyes met hers and they were back on the beach, just the two of them, his body inside hers, his strength on top of her.

'It is.' He nodded, hesitation in his tone. 'But you do not have to decide now.'

'Of course not,' the jeweller agreed. 'I can leave the tray, if you would like to try each for a time?'

Hannah's head spun. Each ring had to feature a diamond of at least ten carats. What must the whole tray be worth?

She didn't want to spend a week prevaricating over which enormous diamond she'd drag around. She just wanted the jeweller to go. She wanted Leonidas to go. Her head was spinning; it was all too much.

We are a one-night stand we can't escape.

He was right, and yet she rejected that description, she recoiled from it with everything she was.

'That's fine.' She shook her head, the beginnings of a throb in her temples. 'This one will be fine.'

She wanted to be alone and perhaps it showed in her voice, because Leonidas was nodding his slow agreement. 'Very well. Thank you for coming, Mr Carter.'

The jeweller left and Hannah watched the helicopter lift off from the cool of the sitting room, taking him from the island and to the mainland of Greece, the sun setting in the background, casting the beautiful machinery in a golden glow.

The day had lived up to the morning's promise. Heat had sizzled and Hannah, having spent so much time preparing for what lay ahead, wanted to simply relax. She'd spied a pool in her explorations the day before and she thought of it longingly now.

'Greg Hassan is scheduled to sit with you today,' Leonidas said as he entered the room.

Hannah's temples throbbed harder. 'Who?' She failed to conceal her weariness.

'Head of security at Stathakis.'

Hannah's throat shifted as she swallowed. 'What do I need to see him for?'

'There are protocols you will need to learn.' He was tense, as if braced for an argument.

'I thought you said this island is far from the mainland, inaccessible to just about anyone...'

He tilted his head in agreement. 'This island is secure, *sigoura*. But there are still protocols to follow and there are always risks.'

His fear was chilling. But it was also very, very sad. She saw the tension in his body, and she wished there were some way she could take it away for him, that she could tell him everything was going to be okay.

She didn't know that it was, but she knew you couldn't live looking over your shoulder.

'Can't you just go through the security stuff with me?'

'You will need to have a relationship with Greg,' he said firmly, his eyes roaming Hannah's face. 'He'll coordinate your movements, and our daughter's, arrange her security detail as she gets older.'

Panic flared inside Hannah. It was all too real and too much. To say she was overwhelmed was an understatement. 'Do you mind if we don't talk about that right now?'

His expression shifted. 'Your safety is important.'

She nodded. 'I know. I'm just—well, I'm worn out, to be honest.'

Concern flashed in his expression. 'Of course. You must be, the day was full and in your condition…'

'It's just a lot to take in.' Her smile was more of a grimace. 'I thought I'd go for a swim and just let it all percolate in my mind.'

'Fine.' He nodded. 'I'll ask Marina to prepare a simple dinner for you, for afterwards.'

Hannah nodded, unable to express why her stomach was swooping. 'Thank you.'

She didn't see Leonidas again that evening. She swam, gently pulling herself through the water, enjoying the lapping of cool against her sun-warmed skin, and then she ate the dinner Mrs Chrisohoidis had prepared—a small pasta dish with some fruit and ice water.

She contemplated going in search of Leonidas afterwards, but the revelations of their conversation from that morning were still sharp inside her.

She slept heavily, which surprised her. When Hannah woke, the sun was up, the sky was bright, and everything felt calmer. Better. Just as her mother had always said it would.

She had a feeling she could handle anything.

She showered, luxuriating in the sensation of the water on her body, lathering herself in the luxury coconut-fragranced products before towelling dry and slipping on a pair of shorts and a loose shirt.

Her stomach rumbled and she put a hand on it unconsciously, smiling as she felt their baby inside her. She looked down, her eyes catching the glinting of her engagement ring and her heart twisted, because she'd worn another man's ring, once upon a time, and she'd become used to seeing that on her finger. Then she'd become used to her hand being empty and bare—she'd been grateful. Grateful she'd found out what Angus was really like before she'd married him.

And now, she was to marry Leonidas. It was a gamble, and she wasn't sure she had the nerves to gamble any more, but here she was, closing her eyes and hoping for the best—all for their daughter's sake. This was all for her.

She had a coffee and some pastries for breakfast and was contemplating a walk on the beach when Leonidas appeared, wearing a similar outfit to the day before.

He wasn't alone.

'Hannah.' He nodded and she wondered if the man behind Leonidas thought the stiff formality of Leonidas's greeting unusual.

'This is Greg Hassan.'

The man in question didn't look anything like what Hannah had imagined. For some reason, 'head of security' conjured images of some kind of black belt muscleman in her mind, someone more like Leonidas, who looked as if they could snap someone with their little finger.

Greg Hassan was on the short side, and slim, with fair skin and bright blue eyes. Hair that had at one time been blond was now balding on top. Hannah was lost in her own thoughts so didn't notice the way he startled a little at the sight of Hannah. But then, he smiled, moving towards her with one hand extended. She met it, belatedly forcing a smile to her own face.

'Miss May, this won't take long.'

In fact, it took hours.

Greg Hassan left some time after noon, and Hannah's head was back to feeling as if it had been through a washing machine.

The island itself had state-of-the-art monitoring, there were panic buttons in each room, and alarms that were activated by unexpected air activity, including drones—the paparazzi had occasionally tried to send drones into the airspace to capture images but the new detection methods effectively made that impossible.

'As for when you travel,' Greg had continued, 'you'll have a team of four bodyguards. One of them will be with you at all times, and another with your child.' He'd smiled reassuringly, as if this were *good* news, but Hannah had felt as if she were having her head held under water.

She was drowning and it hurt.

'As much as possible, we'll coordinate your movements in advance. If you wish to travel to Australia, for example, to see family, we'll send a team out ahead to set up and prepare for your arrival. When your daughter starts school, I presume you'll move to the mainland—' At which point Leonidas had interrupted and said that had not yet been decided. Greg had continued that in the event of their daughter attending a school in Athens, or a major city, the campus would be vetted, and their daughter would wear a watch with an inbuilt panic alarm.

Questions mushroomed inside Hannah's brain, but she hadn't wanted to ask them in front of the security chief.

Leonidas had escorted Greg Hassan from the building and then disappeared to work, leaving Hannah with a million uncertainties scrambling around her brain.

She kept busy, calling her boss, Fergus, and informing him of her decision, and sending a polite, carefully worded email to her aunt, advising her, as a courtesy, that she was pregnant and getting married. She didn't even want to think what the reaction would be. Hannah was careful to leave out any other details—particularly who the groom was.

She texted her flatmates and let them know she wouldn't be coming back, but saying she'd pay rent until they found someone else and she could get back to pack up her room.

It all felt so official, and officially terrifying, but also bizarrely right.

She didn't see Leonidas again until that evening. Hannah stood on the terrace, watching the sun set, her heart lifting as the golden orb dropped, already feeling some kind of soul-deep connection to this land.

She heard his approach, and then she felt his proximity, even though he didn't touch her. It was as simple as the air around her growing thick, sparking with an electrical charge that fired her blood.

She turned slowly to find him there, his eyes locked to her as though he couldn't help himself. But the minute Hannah looked at him, he blinked and looked away, turning his attention to the ocean.

They stood there in silence for a moment, Hannah trying not to react to the throb of awareness low in her abdomen, trying not to act on an impulse to throw herself at him.

As the stars began to shimmer, she found herself remembering the meeting of earlier that day, recalling all the questions that had flooded her. 'You don't travel with a bodyguard.'

'I always have security,' he contradicted.

'Not on New Year's Eve. I didn't see anyone else…'

'My hotel is a fortress when I am there.' He tilted his head towards her, his eyes scanning her face. In the evening light, his sharp features were all harsh angles and planes. 'Additional guards would have been superfluous.'

'Was it like this before the accident?'

'It was no accident,' he responded, whip-sharp.

'Before you lost them,' Hannah corrected.

'Euphemisms? Perhaps if we call it what it is— murder—you will accept the security measures more readily.'

Hannah wasn't sure she agreed.

'And no. Before they were killed, I was stupid and lax with their safety. I was arrogant and thought myself, and everyone around me, invincible, despite my father's connections.'

Hannah moved towards Leonidas, her heart sore for him.

'Isn't that better than living with fear?'

'Living with fear might have kept them alive,' he said, darkly.

'You don't know that.'

'I know they should never have been out wandering the streets.' He ground his teeth. 'And that you and our daughter will never be exposed to that kind of risk…'

Hannah tried not to feel as if she were drowning again. She tried to breathe slowly, to feel the freedom of this island, to understand why he felt as he did.

And she did. She could imagine what pain he must be suffering, and the added layer of guilt. But the picture he was painting was grim. Hannah couldn't imagine not being free to simply wake up and decide to go to the shops, or to visit a friend without having bodyguards do a preparatory security sweep.

'So she'll wear a panic button?' The idea turned Hannah's blood to ice, but then, so did the idea of anything happening to her.

His voice held a warning note. 'At least you'll both be safe.'

His feelings were completely understandable, but Hannah railed against them instinctively. She'd felt loss, she knew its pain well. Losing her parents, then losing her engagement to Angus, she understood what it was like to have everything shift on you.

And yet, being fearless in the face of that was a choice.

'How come there are no pictures of them?'

Leonidas shifted to face Hannah, complex

emotions marring his handsome face. 'What?' The word was sucked from him.

'You were married, what, three years? How come there are no wedding photos? No baby pictures of Brax? If I didn't know about them, I would never have guessed they even existed.'

Leonidas shut his eyes, but not before she saw his grief, his heartache.

'It is not your concern.'

Hannah's insides flexed with acid. Another reminder. His wife and child were off limits. They weren't her concern. His life before her was not up for discussion.

More boundaries. Rules. Distance. It slammed against her and she ground her teeth, the limitations of this like nails under her feet.

'I understand it hurts.' She spoke quietly, lifting a hand to his chest. His heart was pounding. 'But not talking about it doesn't make sense.'

'Please, stop.' She felt his frustration like a whip at the base of her spine.

'Why?'

'Because it is my choice. Because she was my wife and he was my son.' His voice cracked with awful emotion and she swept her eyes shut for a moment, sucking in a breath.

'I know that. And they're a huge part of you, just like our daughter will be.' She carefully kept herself out of that summation.

'But I do not want to discuss them.'

'Why not? Don't you want to remember your son? Don't you want to talk to me—to someone—about his laugh, his smile, his first steps, his night terrors—all the things that made him the little boy he was?'

Leonidas's skin was paler than paper. 'I will never forget my son.'

'I know that,' she said quietly. 'But you can't honour someone by burying their memories.'

Her words hung between them, sharp like an insult, bony and knotty and troublesome and almost too much. She partially rejected the truths of that observation, but she knew from experience what this felt like—she'd been made to stay silent for years, to hold her grief inside, and she'd lost so much of her parents as a result. So many memories she should have been free to relish, to smile about, were gone for ever because of forced disuse.

'He was the light of my life!' he said suddenly. The words were torn from him, animalistic for their pain. He held his ground, staring at her as though she were covering him in acid. 'He was the light of my damned life! Amy and I… I loved her but, God, she drove me crazy and we weren't…in many ways, we weren't well-suited.' He dragged a hand through his hair, his eyes pinpointing Hannah with his grief. 'We'd argued the week before they died. She'd gone to Athens and I was glad.' He groaned, his displeasure at reliving that time in his life evident in every line of his body. 'I was glad because I was sick of fighting with her, sick of disagreeing over unimportant matters. But Brax was my reason for living, my reason for breathing, the reason I would *never* have left Amy.'

Hannah's grief was like dynamite in her chest.

She waited, letting him speak, letting him finish. 'I loved her but Brax was my everything and then he was dead. Because of me.' He dug his fingers into his chest and her eyes dropped to the gesture, to the solid wall of tanned flesh that hid a thundering heart.

'You think I am at risk of forgetting a single thing about him? You think I need to speak to you about my son to remember the way balloons made him laugh riotously, or the way clowns terrified him, or the way he loved to swim and chase butterflies?' His expression softened with grief and love and Hannah held her breath, all of her catching fire with the beauty of that look—of the expression on Leonidas's face.

'Do you think I will ever forget how much he loved strawberries? Cheese? The way he called me Bampás, except he couldn't say it properly so he said Bappmas instead? These things are burned inside my brain, Hannah, whether I speak of them or not.'

It was too real, too raw. She needed to say something, but words failed her. She opened her mouth, searching, seeking, but Leonidas shook his head and then kissed her.

It was a kiss to silence Hannah, a kiss to suck away whatever she'd been going to say and swallow it up, because he'd made it obvious he didn't want her grief, her sympathy, her conversation.

He kissed her, and she resisted for a moment because he was finally opening up to her and she wanted to talk to him, to help him, to hear him. She stiffened in his arms, wanting to push at his chest, to tell him not to run away from this conversation but then he groaned, a guttural sound of such utter, devastating need, and any fight wavered, leaving only surrender.

Surrender and such deep, deep sympathy.

She *understood* the complexity of his emotions.

And the way he kissed her now, she understood what he needed. He wished he didn't want her like this; he'd said as much on the beach, but this flame was burning out of control no matter how they tried to manage it.

'Damn it,' he groaned, swooping down and lifting her up. Regardless of the fact she was five months pregnant, he carried her effortlessly, moving through the mansion with a determined gait.

He shouldered the door to his room open—Hannah hadn't been in here. She looked around, seeing the dark wood, the masculine touches, gathering a brief impression of a space that was huge and elegant before he laid her on the bed, his body coming over hers, his mouth seeking hers as his hands pushed at the waistband of her shorts, lowering them, his hands running over her body.

A gentle breeze rustled in off the Mediterranean, bringing with it salt and warmth. Hannah lifted herself up, kissing him as her hands pushed at his shirt, guiding it over his chest, up to his head. He broke the kiss so she could remove it and then she lay back, breathless, her eyes running over his chest.

The room was dark, but she could see enough. She drank in the sight of him as quickly as she could because he kissed her again, his tongue flicking hers, his hands worshipping her body.

He brought his mouth lower, pushing at her shirt, lifting it to her throat so he could take one of her breasts into his mouth, his tongue swirling over a nipple until she bucked beneath him, stars flashing in her eyelids.

'God,' she moaned, digging her heels into the

bed, arching her back, begging him to take her, to thrust inside her.

His mouth moved to her other breast and his fingers took over, his palm feeling the weight of her breast, his thumb and forefinger teasing her nipple until she was a puddle of whimpering nerves.

'Please,' she husked, running her nails down his back.

His arousal was hard between her legs; his knee nudged her thighs further apart and then he thrust into her, the ache unmistakable, the same urge overrunning them both. She felt his need and mirrored the depth of it.

She lifted herself onto her elbows, finding his mouth, pulling his lower lip between her teeth and biting down on it, so he let out a sharp sound of shock and then a groan as he pushed her head back to the mattress, his kiss a complete domination and sublime pleasure.

Only she wanted more, she wanted to be in control of this. She kissed him back, just as hard, needing him to understand her—this. Needing to reassure him in some way.

She moved herself over his arousal, her breath pinched, her body screaming in relief.

Hannah's heart hammered against her ribs and pleasure burst, touching every single part of her, until she was all fire and flame, no room for thoughts and feelings, doubts and uncertainties.

Concerns of security, the future, their relationship, his grief, her loss, they all disappeared. What room was there for anything when there was this pleasure in life?

Her breathing was rhythmic and he couldn't take his eyes off her.

Her vibrant red hair spread over his crisp white pillows, glowing like copper, and his gut throbbed painfully.

Leonidas Stathakis had tormented himself for the four years after his wife's death, staying celibate even when his body had begged him to relent, even when he'd wanted to lose himself in a willing woman's arms.

He hadn't.

He hadn't given in, until he'd seen Hannah and something inside him had begun to beat, a drum he could no longer ignore.

And it was still beating, but harder and faster now. With Hannah under his roof, it was impossible to ignore this; just as she'd said.

Theirs wasn't a normal marriage, but they did have this, and suddenly, Leonidas didn't want to fight it any more.

He watched her sleep, her beautiful, pregnant body naked to his hungry gaze, and he gave up fighting altogether. Perhaps in the morning he'd feel differently, but, for now, Leonidas allowed himself to curve his body behind hers, to place an arm possessively over her stomach and to fall asleep for the first time in a long time with a woman in his bed.

CHAPTER TEN

HANNAH WOKE, STRETCHING until her back connected with something hard and warm behind her. Her heart was racing, the meeting with Greg Hassan the day before having left a lingering sense of anxiety in her so that alarm was her first emotion, followed swiftly by something much warmer, much more tempting, when she corkscrewed in the bed and realised where she was, and who she was with.

Leonidas.

And he was awake.

Staring at her.

His naked body was not a mystery to her, and yet this was the first time she'd woken up beside him, or any man, and a hint of self-consciousness made her cheeks blush.

'I fell asleep,' she said quietly, her eyes dropping to his chest. 'I'm sorry.'

She didn't see the way his brows curved reflexively into a frown.

'Why are you apologising?'

Hannah lifted her gaze to his. 'I don't know. I guess I would have thought you'd want your space. Or to not have me here.'

His frown deepened and there was silence for several beats. 'I would have thought so, too.'

More silence.

'You were right, on the beach, Hannah. There is something between us. This chemistry.' His eyes were hollow when they met hers. 'I don't want to fight it any more.'

Her blood hammered inside her, hope was rolling inside her but she stayed completely still, watching him, listening.

'I have been single a long time. Single by choice. I have no idea how to do this. And I don't want to hurt you.' His expression showed his doubts on that score.

'Why do you think you're going to?'

His face bore a mask of wariness.

'I don't want you to think that great sex is more meaningful than that.'

Hannah swallowed, her brain turning his words over, making sense of them. He was afraid—afraid to risk falling in love, afraid to risk getting close to anyone. She understood that. He'd loved and lost. He was gun-shy now. But opening himself up to their intimacy was one thing—it was a definite step, and for now that was enough.

Hannah smiled slowly, her eyes sparkling in a way that made Leonidas draw in an audible breath.

'Don't worry, Leonidas Stathakis,' she said, pushing at his shoulder so he fell back on the mattress and straddling him at the same time, surprising him so his eyes flared. 'I'm very happy to just use you for sex for now.'

His laugh was throaty, his expression shifting into one of complete fascination.

'Is that right?' She took his erection in her hands, feeling his strength, running her fingertips over his length, her smile pure sensual heat.

'Oh, yes.' She pushed up on her haunches, then brought herself over his arousal, taking him deep inside her but so slowly that he dug his fingertips into her hips and pulled her the rest of the way, his eyes holding hers.

She bit down on her lip and arched her back and he pulled up then, sitting, wrapping his arms around her, sucking one of her nipples in his mouth, flicking it with his tongue. Her breasts were so sensitive that his touch was like an arrow firing right into her central nervous system. She cried out, his name heavy on her lips, her nails on his shoulders, and he held her tighter, thrusting into her. With her on top, he reached different places, and she felt a different kind of explosion building, more intense somehow, taking over her body.

'Leonidas.' She ran her fingers through his hair and then cupped his face, pulling him away from her chest so she could kiss his mouth, and he kissed her back, hard, their tongues duelling, even as he shifted their body weight, spinning her, rolling her onto her back so he could take even more of her, thrusting into her hungrily, deep, hard and fast, and Hannah pushed her hands up, wrapping her fingers around the bedhead and holding on for dear life, and pleasure threatened to explode her out of this world.

He leaned forward, catching her hands, peeling them off the bedhead, lacing his fingers through hers and, as on the beach, he pinned them above her head, so his hair-roughened torso was hard against hers and every single cell in her body reacted to this tactile contact, to his nearness.

Her orgasm splintered her apart and it was Leonidas who put her back together, each gentle murmur, his voice speaking in Greek, his kiss gentle now, soft, reassuring as she flew straight into the abyss.

'You don't think this is overkill?' Hannah murmured, surveying the island from the vantage point he'd driven her to. From here, she could see so much more than the house, including a full golf course, a helipad as well as the airstrip, and in the distance what looked to be a whole little village. There was a jetty, too, and another yacht was tied to it—not as large as the one in Capri, but still what Hannah had to imagine would be classed as a 'superyacht', beautiful and shimmering white.

'What is?'

'This island.' She couldn't help the smile that teased her lips. She'd woken that morning, in his bed, and something had felt easier between them. She knew there were demons driving him, controlling him, but they weren't the sum total of Leonidas Stathakis.

He shrugged nonchalantly. 'You don't like it?'

'Oh, I like it very much,' she contradicted, rolling her eyes a little. 'But who wouldn't? I just don't think I'll ever get used to living like this.'

'It's just a bigger home than you're used to.'

Hannah laughed at that, lifting the takeaway coffee cup she'd brought with her, sipping on it, wondering if she'd ever con herself into enjoying decaf. 'By about three thousand times. And then there's the expansive private beach.'

He looked at her, a smile pulling at his lips, and her heart turned over because he was really, exceptionally handsome, and when he smiled, it was as if someone had turned the music up full volume.

Her eyes dropped to his lips and her pulse gushed through her body, stirring heat in her veins and anticipation low down in her abdomen.

'I haven't thought about it in a long time,' he said simply. 'It's just the island, to me.'

'Naturally.' She was still smiling as she turned her eyes back to the view. 'Did you grow up here?'

'No.'

'Where, then?'

'Athens, mainly—Kifissia. My father's offices were in the city.' The words were flat, carefully blanked of any emotion.

But Hannah felt it. She felt it rolling off him in waves, crashing against her, just like the ocean to the shore. She swallowed, butterflies in her tummy making her hesitate a little.

'What happened with him?'

'You don't know?'

She shrugged, awkwardly. 'I had to look you up on the Internet, to work out how to contact you.'

His eyes roamed hers, probing thoughtfully.

'I mean, I saw a headline, but I didn't click into it.'

'Why not?' His expression showed genuine surprise.

'Because it kind of gives me the creeps. Doesn't it you?'

He arched a brow, clearly not comprehending.

'Well, it's not really any of my business. It seemed private to you and your family.' She wrinkled her nose, lost in thought. 'I guess there's a lot about you out there, and your brother, and your dad. But what kind of stalker would I be to read it?'

'Your stalkerishness is someone else's due diligence,' he said with a quirk of his lips. 'What if I'm some kind of pathological cheat?'

'Are you?' She turned her face to his, her eyes scanning his features.

'No.' The word was sombre.

Silence arced between them, electric and sharp. He seemed to be peeling her away, looking deep inside her, even though the question had been Hannah's.

'And see? I believe you.' Her own voice was a little husky.

'Why?'

Hannah replaced her coffee cup in the golf cart they'd been touring the island in, then spun around to face him, so their bodies were almost touching. 'Because you've never lied to me, Leonidas.'

His expression tightened imperceptibly, his jaw square.

'You told me on New Year's Eve that we'd only ever be one night. You didn't make big promises to get me into bed. You were honest. You were honest with me this morning. I don't think you know how to lie.'

Leonidas looked beyond her, to the horizon. 'Honesty is generally the best policy, is it not?'

'Yes.' Her smile was uneven.

'I would have thought, having learned of your fiancé's infidelity, you would be slow to trust anyone.'

'So would I.' Her voice was a little shaky. 'But you're nothing like Angus. You're nothing like anyone I've ever met.'

At this, Leonidas's expression tightened, and she understood that he was closing himself off, that she'd moved them into territory he couldn't yet traverse.

'What did he do, anyway?'

'Who?'

'Your father.'

'Ah.' He expelled a slow breath, as though fortifying himself for what would come next.

'I gather he's in prison?'

'Serving a twenty-year sentence.'

'I'm so sorry.'

'What for? Prison is where criminals should be.'

'Yes, but he's your dad…'

'Not any more.'

Hannah frowned. 'You hate him?'

'Yes.'

She nodded thoughtfully. 'Why?'

'My father turned his back on the Stathakis Corporation. He almost destroyed what my grandfather, great-grandfather, and his father had spent their lifetimes building. Ancient, proud shipping lines that funded investments in foreign hotels and then hedge funds—our operations were crippled because of him.'

'How? Surely your company's too big for any one man to destroy?'

'He began to fund the mob, Hannah.' His eyes were haunted now, furious too, zipping with tightly coiled emotions. 'My father—who was richer than Croesus—didn't just want money and the lifestyle it afforded. He wanted power. No, not power; he wanted people to be afraid of him. He wanted notoriety and reach.'

'I can't even imagine what drives a man to think like that,' she said with a gentle shake of her head. 'How could he have even met that element?'

'It's everywhere. Casinos, bars, commercial investments.' Leonidas expelled a harsh breath. 'He was always enamoured of that lifestyle. I'm only surprised it took so long for him to be arrested.'

'That must have been so hard for you.'

'I think of myself as a strong person but I have no idea how I would have coped without Thanos.' The confession surprised her, and softened her, all at once. 'Investigators from every country in which we do business went over our records with a fine-tooth comb. We lost anything that had been used to fund crime. Despite the fact Thanos and I had been groomed from a young age, at our grandfather's knee, to love our company like a member of this family, to work hard to better it, we had to watch it being pulled apart, piece by piece, to see it crumble and fail.'

Sadness clouded Hannah's eyes; the image he was painting was one that was loaded with grief.

'What did you do?'

His expression was laced with determination and she thought of a phoenix, rising from the ashes. 'We cut the failing businesses, sold them off piece by piece, got what we could for them and recouped by aggressively buying into emerging markets. It was a high-risk strategy, but what did we have to lose?'

Hannah felt the conversational ground shift a little beneath them. She knew there was danger ahead, but, again, something had changed, there was more clarity, as if a valve had given way and now there was a clear flow of comprehension, an understanding.

'You said Amy was murdered in a vendetta against your father?'

His features tightened, and his jet-black eyes glittered with hatred—not for her, but for the men responsible. 'Yes.'

It was like pulling fingernails, she knew. He

didn't want to do this, and yet, he wasn't hiding from her, even when it was causing him pain.

'He cut a deal with a prosecutor. Multiple life sentences were reduced to a twenty-year term, all because he handed over the names of his associates.' Leonidas's contempt was apparent, his lips little more than a snarl. 'He didn't, for one second, think of how that would affect us—those of us out here, living in this world.'

'Perhaps he was just trying to do the right thing?'

Leonidas surprised Hannah then, because he smiled—a smile that was tinged with grief. 'You see the world through the veneer of your goodness,' he said after a moment. 'You think because your motivations are pure and good, everyone else's must always be?'

'No.' She frowned; it wasn't that at all.

'Yes,' he insisted. 'How else could you have become engaged to a man who was cheating on you? You trust and you forgive.'

'Is that a bad thing?'

He was quiet, staring at her for several beats. 'I hope not.'

Hannah expelled a soft breath. 'Maybe I do give people more than their fair chance. But I also see the truth—I know what people are capable of, Leonidas. I've seen it. I've felt it.'

She looked away from him then, her eyes gravitating to the yacht as it bobbed on the surface of the Mediterranean. Everything was clear and pristine, and so very beautiful, like stepping into a postcard.

Leonidas's fingers curled around her chin, gently pulling her back to face him.

'He hurt you?'

Hannah's eyes widened, and it took her a moment to think who he was referring to.

'He was my fiancé, and he had an affair… Of course that hurt. But it wasn't him alone; it was her, too. It was the fact that two of the people who were supposed to love me most in the world had been happy to betray me with one another.' She shuddered, the shock of that moment one she wasn't sure she'd ever get over. 'It wasn't losing Angus. It was the whole situation.'

His eyes devoured Hannah's face, tasting her expression, digesting its meaning. 'Have you spoken to her?'

Hannah shook her head. 'I couldn't. I can't. I don't know what I'd say. Growing up, our relationship wasn't always…easy.'

'Why not?' he pushed, and she had a glimpse of his formidable analytical skills. She felt his determination to comprehend her words, to seek out what was at the root of them.

'She was competitive, and frankly insecure. Her mother—Aunt Cathy—spurred her on, making comments about how we looked, or about grades.' Hannah sighed. 'I never bought into it. I mean, we're all our own person, right? Run your own race. That's what my mum used to say.' Her smile was nostalgic, and then, it slipped from her lips like the sun being consumed by a storm cloud. 'But my aunt…'

He waited, patiently, for her to continue. Hannah searched for the words.

'She measured us against each other non-stop.'

'And your cousin didn't measure up?'

Hannah's eyes shot to Leonidas's. 'I didn't say that.'

'No, you are being deliberately tactful on that score.'

There was enough praise in that observation to bring heat to Hannah's cheeks, but she denied it.

'I'm not being coy. I just don't think like that. Michelle struggled at school; I didn't. I suspect she has some kind of undiagnosed dyslexia— no matter how much time we spent going over things, she found the comprehension impossible. I think she wasn't able to read clearly, and covered it by acting uninterested.'

'You mentioned this to your aunt?'

Hannah nodded. 'Once. She was furious.' Hannah's expression was unconsciously pained, her features pinched tight as her gaze travelled back towards the ocean.

'And you, in comparison, excelled at your studies?'

Hannah nodded slowly. 'Some people respond well to the school system, others don't. I'm lucky in that I'm one of the former.'

'And a lifetime of feeling compared to has made you downplay your natural abilities even now, here, to me.'

She startled at that insight. 'It's the truth.'

'It is also the truth to say you are intelligent, and I would bet my fortune on the fact you worked hard at school, too.' He softened his tone a little, but didn't quit his line of questioning. 'Isn't it possible that your aunt resented how well you did, compared to Michelle? That she couldn't get help for her daughter because it would be admitting she was, in some way, inferior?'

'If I'm right and Michelle had a learning difficulty of sorts then she could have been helped, and achieved far better results than she did.'

He dipped his head in a silent concession. 'But your aunt didn't want to pursue that. And so, instead, she took away your dreams, condemning you to a life of mediocrity so her own daughter would look better in comparison?'

Hannah sucked in a sharp breath, his words like acid rain against her flesh. 'I don't think you could call my life mediocre...'

'You should have been studying law, poised

to move into the career you really wanted. And your aunt should have been supporting you. This is what you meant, when you said you have felt what people are capable of?'

She opened her mouth to deny it, but he was too insightful. Too right. She shrugged instead, lifting her shoulders and turning away from him.

'Where was your uncle in all of this?'

'Gary?'

'You speak of your aunt and your cousin, but I have not heard you say his name once.'

'He worked a lot. We weren't close.'

'And yet he must have known how his wife was behaving. He did nothing?'

'It's not like that. Aunt Cathy isn't a monster. It's complicated.'

'How?'

Hannah shook her head thoughtfully. 'It was so long ago, and I don't really know anything for certain. It's more just things I've picked up from throwaway comments. I think she was very close to my dad—her brother. And when Mum entered the scene, Aunt Cathy was jealous. Hurt. My mum was…' Hannah's smile was melancholy and she closed her eyes, seeing Eleanor May as she'd been in life—so vital, so beautiful. 'She was a pretty amazing woman. A diplomat for the United Nations, well travelled, passionate, funny, and so stunning.'

'So this is where you get it from,' he murmured, the compliment wrapping around her, filling her with gold dust.

Hannah smiled slowly, memories of her past pulling at her. 'I used to love watching her get ready for parties. She had this long, dark brown hair, like chocolate, that fell to her waist. She would coil it up into a bun, high on the top of her head, so that whatever dangly earrings she chose to wear would take your breath away.' Hannah felt him come closer, his body heat and proximity firing something in her blood.

'And she and Dad were so happy together. They used to laugh, all the time. I was just a kid when they died, but I'll never forget them, I'll never forget how lucky I was to have them as my example in life.'

He was quiet, but it didn't matter. Some part of Leonidas had slipped into Hannah, forming a part of her, so she understood—she understood his silence equated to disapproval of Aunt Cathy, and her inability to let Hannah properly grieve.

And long-held needs to defend Aunt Cathy were difficult to ignore. 'Cathy and Gary weren't like my parents. They married young, because she was pregnant. She lost the baby but they stayed together and it always felt a bit like they resented each other.'

She turned to face him then, her chest heavy

with the myriad sadnesses of the past. 'I don't want our marriage to be like that, Leonidas.'

Her eyes raked his face and she chewed her lower lip thoughtfully as he stared at her, his eyes unshifting from hers, his expression impossible to interpret.

'I was wrong about you.' Leonidas's words came out hoarse, thickened by regret.

'When?'

'I presumed you did not know enough of grief to counsel me, to offer me any thoughts on my own experiences. That was incredibly arrogant.' He lifted a hand, running it over her hair, his attention shifting higher, as if mesmerised by the auburn shades there, flecked with gold. 'I downplayed what you have been through because I couldn't believe anyone could feel loss like mine.'

'It's not like yours,' she said softly, gently, her heart breaking. 'No grief is the same. I can't imagine what it's like to lose your partner, nor your child.' She shook her head sadly from side to side. 'I'm five months pregnant and the idea of anything ever happening to our daughter fills me with a kind of rage I can't put into words.' Her lips twisted in a humourless smile. 'You must be a mix of anger and fury and pain and disbelief all the time.' She swallowed, rallying her thoughts. 'You don't need to apologise to me. I understood what you meant.'

'But I didn't understand you,' he insisted. 'I didn't realise that beyond the somewhat sanitised phrase of "orphan" are all the memories of parents you loved, parents who made you happy and secure, parents who were replaced by an inferior substitute—an insecure and competitive woman who spent her life trying to diminish you.'

Hannah's lips pulled downwards, as she tried to reconcile his vision of Aunt Cathy.

'You should have studied law,' he said, simply. 'And anyone who loved you would have pushed you to do that, supporting you, encouraging you, making it easier—not harder—to pursue your dreams.'

Hannah's heart turned over in her chest, because he was right. Even Angus hadn't said as much to her.

'Your parents left you money. That could have been used to fund your studies.'

'I couldn't access it yet, not for another two years.'

'But a bank would have loaned against that expectation, if your aunt and uncle couldn't cover your expenses in the interim. There were ways for you to live your dreams but she held you back because she didn't want you to succeed.'

Something sparked in Hannah's chest because he was right, and she'd made excuses for Cathy and Gary all her life and she didn't want to do it any more.

'I miss my mum and dad every day,' she said, simply, focussing on the only kernel of good she could grasp at. 'Especially now.' She ran a hand over her stomach, thinking of the daughter growing inside her, and love burst in her soul.

The air between them resonated with understanding, with compassion, and then Hannah blinked away, moving her focus to the vista before them.

Their conversation was serious, and yet she felt a shifting lightness in her heart, a sense of newness. Perhaps it was simply the beauty of the day, or looking down over the horizon and seeing so much that fascinated her, so much to explore, but she found herself smiling.

'What's down there?' She nodded towards the village she could see in the distance. 'I thought this was a private island.'

'It is. That's the staff quarters.'

'Staff quarters?'

His smile was teasing. 'Where did you think all the people in the house went to at night?'

'I didn't think about it,' she said, and he smiled then, a smile that was natural and easy and that made her pulse feel as if it had hitched a ride on a roller coaster and were zipping and whooshing through her body.

'There are about fifteen gardeners, Mrs Chrisohoidis, her husband Andreo, who over-sees the island, the domestic staff, chefs, and I have two personal assistants based out of the is-land for when I need to work.'

Hannah's eyes flew wide. 'Seriously?'

'And their families,' he said, still smiling, the words lightly mocking.

She shook her head from side to side, wonder-ing at how anyone could have this kind of money.

'It takes a team to manage all this.' He gestured with his palm to the island.

She nodded. 'And then the yacht crew, too?'

He nodded. 'They stay on board, though there are dorms for when the boat is here over winter.'

'You must spend a fortune in salaries.'

'I suppose I do.' He wasn't smiling now, but he was looking at her with a heat that simmered her blood. He lifted a hand to her hair once more, tucking it behind her ear slowly, watchfully.

'There's the security team, as well,' he said, and she felt his past pulling him deep into a rag-ing ocean.

'Greg Hassan lives here?'

'Greg lives in Athens. He oversees Stathakis Corp, including my brother Thanos's security arrangements, and our company procedures. He has a manager on the island, and there are thir-teen guards permanently placed here.'

'Thirteen?' She exhaled. 'Security guards?'

'It used to be only four,' he said nonchalantly.

'But because of me it's thirteen?'

'Because of you, and because of her.' He dropped a hand to Hannah's stomach, and right at that moment one of the little popping sensations Hannah had become used to reared to life, and Leonidas's eyes widened in wonder.

'Did she just kick me?'

Hannah laughed, but there was a sting of happy tears against her eyelids. 'She's telling you we don't need anything like that kind of security.'

'I think she's giving me a high five of agreement.'

Hannah laughed and Leonidas did, too. She had no way of knowing how long it had been since he'd felt genuine amusement, or the occurrence might have taken her breath away even more than the sound did on its own.

Hannah lay with her head on Leonidas's chest, in the small hours of the next day, listening to his heart. It beat slow and steady in sleep. She lay there, her naked body close to his, their limbs tangled with the crisp white sheets, their bodies spent, her body round with the baby they'd made, and she smiled.

Because there was such randomness in this, and yet such perfection, too.

How could she have known that one night of unplanned sensual heat would lead to this? She lay with her head on his chest, listening to the solid beating of his heart, and admitted to herself there was nowhere on earth she'd rather be.

CHAPTER ELEVEN

'YOU'RE GETTING MARRIED?'

Thanos's voice came to Leonidas from a long way away.

'Where are you?' Leonidas stretched his long legs out in front of himself, crossing them at the ankles.

'Somewhere over the Atlantic.'

'You're going to New York?'

'It's model week.' Leonidas could hear his brother's grin, and experience told him that in approximately twenty-four hours there'd be tabloid headlines about Thanos's latest stunning conquest. 'Did you say you're getting married?'

Leonidas's eyes drifted to the window of his study, and beyond it, to where Hannah was lying beside the pool. The bathing costume was really just a couple of scraps of Lycra, and his fingers itched to remove it.

'Yes.'

'*You're* getting married?'

Leonidas grimaced. 'On Friday.'

'As in three days away *Friday*?'

'Yes.'

'*Christós.* I didn't realise you were seeing anyone.'

'I'm not. I wasn't.' He swept his eyes shut, his stomach clenching painfully. 'It's not like that.'

'So what is it like?'

Leonidas's chest felt as if it were being scooped out, replaced with acid. 'She's pregnant.'

Silence.

It stretched for so long that Leonidas thought they might have lost reception. The phones on their state-of-the-art jets were good, but not one hundred per cent reliable.

'Thanos?'

'I'm sorry, I'm just surprised. I thought you'd sworn off women for life.'

'So did I.'

'And yet?'

'And yet,' Leonidas agreed, his eyes roaming her body with a hunger that was not a part of him. He'd given up on fighting this, on fighting Hannah. She was breathing herself into his soul, and taking over small parts of him, forming his building blocks back into shape. Except for his heart, which would always be locked away, re-served for Amy and Brax.

The rest of him, he could share. Especially if it made her smile the way she had been.

'When? I mean to say, when will you have this baby?'

'She's due in four months.'

Thanos let out a low whistle. 'So you're marrying her for custody?'

The description turned Leonidas's stomach. 'I'm marrying her for security.'

A moment of silence and then, gently, 'Leonidas, the man who killed them is locked up for life. He'll never get out. There's no reason to think he wasn't acting alone.'

'It's organised crime. Do you really think he'd have operated without instruction?'

'Yes,' Thanos spoke swiftly. 'I think he was a lunatic, angry that our father had turned on his brother and so he took that out on you—an eye for an eye. There is no risk now.'

'Would you bet someone's life on that, Thanos? Would you bet the life of an innocent woman you were too weak to resist and that of her unborn child?'

More silence, and eventually, 'No.'

Leonidas didn't realise until that moment how badly he'd needed to hear that. 'Here with me, on the island, she is safe. Our child will be safe.'

'What's she like?'

'She's…' Leonidas tried to put into words a hint of Hannah, but it proved hard for some reason. 'She's nice. You'll like her.'

Thanos's disapproval came across in his silence. 'Nice?'

'Yes, nice. What's wrong with "nice"?'

Thanos was quiet. 'Does she know about Amy?'

Leonidas stiffened. 'Yes.'

'Leo.' Thanos rarely used the diminutive version of Leonidas's name. It slipped out, the boy-hood moniker coming naturally to him now. 'You don't think it's a bit of an extreme way to keep someone safe? You couldn't just give her a security detail?'

Leonidas was surprised to realise he hadn't even considered that. Not for a moment. But he understood his reasoning. Having lost Amy and Brax, he couldn't risk anything else happening to the mother of his child, and the only way to be sure of that was to have her within eyesight. He and Amy had fought—often. They'd begun spending more and more time apart. He'd missed Brax like anything but he'd relished his space from Amy, even when he'd known he loved her— or that he had loved her once and needed to honour that love, for the sake of their child.

But he'd been careless, letting her go without taking an interest in how she was spending her time. He hadn't seen the danger and they'd paid the ultimate price.

No. Hannah would be by his side, 'til death do them part. And if they were separated and he couldn't protect her, then he'd make sure she had an army at her disposal.

'A detail wouldn't have been enough. It's my job to keep them safe.'

'I see.' It was clear Thanos didn't agree, though. 'And is this what she wants?'

Leonidas stood, moving to the window, and his legs felt a little like jelly when he thought about what Hannah might want. Perhaps she caught a hint of his movement in her peripheral vision, or perhaps she felt the tug of him in that strange way she had, but she lifted her gaze to the window of his study, lifting her sunglasses from her head so she could pierce him, through the glass, with the intensity of her emerald eyes.

His pulse slammed inside him.

'She agrees it's for the best.'

Thanos was quiet for a moment. 'It all sounds very sensible and safe, then.'

Leonidas nodded, but his insides were clenching in a way that wasn't even remotely sensible.

'Maybe you could take over negotiations with Kosta Carinedes now that you're about to be married with a kid. That's the kind of respectability he's looking for.'

Leonidas stiffened—the reality of that still difficult to contemplate. And though Thanos had obviously been joking, he was quick to retort, 'There is no way on earth I'm telling anyone who doesn't need to know about Hannah and our daughter. I plan on keeping this secret as long as I can.'

There was safety in secrecy.

Hannah smiled up at him, and lifted her hand, motioning for him to come to her, then pointing to the water.

He shook his head on autopilot, the last vestiges of restraint reminding him that there needed to be some boundaries, some restrictions.

She shrugged, standing up slowly, unfurling her petite frame and turning her back on him. She reached behind her as he watched, pulling on the string of her bikini top and lifting it over her head. Her hair, shimmering like a flame in the afternoon sunshine, ignited down her back.

He held his breath as she turned once more and blew him a kiss, her smile contagious, spreading over his lips, exploding out of her like diamond dust. And then she eased herself into the pool, her beautiful, pale breasts only half covered by the water.

He disconnected the call to Thanos, threw his phone on his desk and was already stripping his clothes as he made his way to the deck.

It was just a swim on a very hot day, nothing more.

Leonidas told himself he was simply doing what Hannah deserved. That it was easy for him to deliver on her dreams and that someone should do that for her, after everything she'd lost.

She was marrying one of the richest men in the world—she could have anything she wanted in life and Leonidas was going to make sure she knew that.

He couldn't give her his heart, he couldn't give her the version of happily ever after she wanted, but he could spoil her with every material possession so that she never noticed there was a gaping void inside her chest.

He told himself a thousand and one things but as he observed Hannah with undisguised interest, watched the way her face glowed with happiness and wonderment, he knew there was something more base in his reasons for bringing her here, to Paris.

The idea had come to him while they were swimming, earlier that day. They were marrying for somewhat pragmatic reasons, but that didn't mean he couldn't make some of her dreams come true. And she had always wanted to see Paris, had grown up staring at a tourist souvenir of the Eiffel Tower, and he could give her the real thing. He'd wanted her to have it.

Why?

Because it had mattered to him.

Because he could.

Because someone should spoil Hannah May.

'Leonidas.' She turned to face him, tears in her eyes. 'It's so much more beautiful than I'd imagined.'

Their penthouse hotel room looked over the glowing construction of the city's heart, the Eiffel Tower. He handed her a glass of non-alcoholic champagne, moving closer to her, still unable to tear his gaze from her face.

'Many locals would beg to differ.'

But even his cynicism couldn't dampen her mood. 'Then they're crazy.' She grinned. 'I've never seen anything more beautiful.'

'Haven't you?' His voice was thick and guilt rolled through him. He banked it down. This wasn't about him and Amy and Brax and the mess that was his life. This was about Hannah—she deserved to be happy, she deserved to feel joy, she deserved this. And he wasn't going to ruin it by brooding and regretting.

She lifted her eyes to his and heat seared him, as it had the first night they met, as it always did.

'I guess you come here all the time. You're probably used to it.'

He skipped his gaze to the Eiffel Tower thoughtfully. 'Often enough.'

'I can't imagine seeing it as just another land-mark. It's extraordinary.'

As she looked at it the hour struck and the tower went from glowing gold to glistening with silver and starlight. Hannah drew in a sharp breath and moved closer, through the billowing curtains and onto the small Juliet balcony with an unrivalled view of the tourist favourite.

'Tomorrow I want to go right to the top,' she said with a broad grin, turning back to face him.

'Why wait until tomorrow?' he prompted, holding a hand out to her.

'Because it's eight o'clock. Surely it's not open to visitors?'

'It's open until midnight,' he said with a smile.

'Then what are we waiting for?' she asked breathlessly, yet he didn't move. He stared at her, drinking in the sight of her like this, and something shifted in his gut—hope, lightness, release.

He ignored it, taking her hand and squeezing it tight in his own. 'Not a thing. Let's go, *agape mou.*'

Hannah slept with a smile on her face and woke with it still drifting over her lips. Her sleeping mind had been full of all the dreams that Leonidas had made a reality. The surprise trip to Paris—touching down in his private jet at Charles de Gaulle and being whisked through the ancient city in his sleek black limousine.

She hadn't been able to speak, she'd been too thrilled, too fascinated, intent on catching every detail she possibly could. She'd craned forward in her seat, staring at the city as it passed and her heart had begun to throb and twist and race for how much the city lived up to her every dream.

And for how close she felt to her mother here. It had been Eleanor's favourite city—she'd spent a lot of time in Paris for the UN and had come home speaking about it, bringing the city to life in a young Hannah's imagination.

The Stathakis Hotel was in the heart of this thriving metropolis, poised on the edge of the Seine, showcasing views in one direction of the Eiffel Tower and in the other of the Arc de Triomphe, and in between all the winding streets and tiny little houses that made this city so singularly unique.

The penthouse was exquisite, just like the one on Chrysá Vráchia, only it was different—there was more of a flavour of France in its styling. The artwork was done by the hand of famous Impressionists, the furniture a little more elaborate and baroque; everything about it was sumptuous and romantic.

And it had been waiting for them when they arrived.

It had all been so perfect and Hannah had almost been able to ignore the presence of the security officers who'd accompanied them on the flight and through the streets of Paris. Constantly walking a discreet distance behind but always there, always watching and waiting.

And despite the joy of this city, a frisson of alarm travelled down her spine, a hint of worry at what had befallen Amy and Brax and the threats Leonidas seemed to imagine were still out there.

She turned over in bed, lifting a finger to his shoulder and tracing an invisible circle distractedly across his tanned flesh.

His eyes lifted and he turned to face her, a look on his face she couldn't interpret before he smiled.

Her heart turned over in her chest.

'Bonjour.'

His smile widened. *'Bonjour, mademoiselle.'*

'I like it here,' she said simply, dropping her head to his chest but keeping her gaze trained squarely on the picture-perfect Eiffel Tower beyond the window. It was a perfect day—a bright blue sky called to her and Hannah was already excited to explore this ancient city.

'I thought you might.'

And so he'd arranged this. Something pulled inside her chest—pleasure—and she smiled softly. 'Is it possible, Leonidas, that you are a romantic at heart?'

His chest slowed, his body completely still. 'No.' The word was like thunder in the midst of a sunny day. She pushed up to look at him, not cowed by the stern expression on his face. A week ago, she would have bitten her tongue, but something had shifted between them; she was different now. He'd made her different.

Hannah liked to think she wasn't the same girl who'd agreed to marry Angus, who'd taken her aunt's decrees as gospel. She bit down on her lower lip, watching him, thinking, and then said, 'How did you meet her?'

His eyes dropped to hers, his expression unreadable. She wondered if he was going to plead 'off limits', as he had at the start, but he didn't.

Though it clearly gave him no pleasure and considerable pain, he spoke slowly, quietly, the words dredged from deep within him. 'Through my brother.'

Silence. She didn't fill it.

'Thanos has a broad social circle.' Scepticism filled the words. 'Amy had just started modelling. She got pulled along to a party by some friends. I happened to be there.'

'She was a model?'

Leonidas nodded. 'She was beautiful and I was smitten.' His smile was dismissive but jealousy surged inside Hannah. She knew how petty that was. The poor woman had died and it was not for Hannah to envy her anything.

'Did you date for long before marrying?'

'No,' he laughed softly. 'I am not a patient man.

When I see something I want I go after it.' His frown was another storm cloud on the horizon. 'We married quickly, privately, and before we really knew much about one another.'

Hannah tilted her head to the side, watching him. 'You say that as though it's a bad thing.'

'It can be,' he said thoughtfully.

Curiosity got the better of Hannah. 'Was she different from what you imagined?'

Leonidas flicked his gaze to Hannah's, his eyes showing torment. 'I loved her.' The words were defensive. 'But we weren't capable of making each other happy.'

Sympathy scored deep into Hannah's heart.

'I thought a baby might be the answer to that. I convinced her to fall pregnant, and by then she was so afraid of losing me I think she would have borne me a football team if I'd asked it of her.' He shook his head from side to side, anger in the tight lines of his lips.

'Why weren't you happy?' she asked curiously.

He expelled a soft sigh. 'Neither of us was happy.' He moved his gaze to the window, looking through it without seeing. 'Amy loved a certain lifestyle.'

'Money?'

He grimaced. 'Money was not the issue. Partying was. She loved to go out, to be seen, to be adored. She fell into my brother's crowd for a reason.'

Sympathy shifted inside Hannah's chest. 'And you're not like that?'

'I never have been. Thanos is the "playboy prince of Europe" and that suits him. He lives his life in the fast lane—life can never be loud enough, fast enough, drunk enough.' His smile showed affection. 'He's a tornado. And he attracts tornados.'

'Like Amy.'

'Yes. Like Amy. She was much more at home with his friends. I couldn't make her happy.'

'But you loved her.'

A heavy beat of silence throbbed between them. 'Yes.' He turned to face her. 'And I refused to let our marriage fail.'

Hannah expelled a soft sigh. 'You can't beat yourself up for things not having been perfect. I sometimes think life is a knot full of different threads. Some of them happy, some of them profoundly sad, but they all form a part of you.' She pressed a finger to his chest.

Leonidas lay back and gave his fiancée the full force of his attention. 'And you think you would have been happy with him?'

Hannah considered that for a moment. 'I think I would have been free with Angus. Free of my aunt and uncle and their low expectations, free of Michelle's jealousy. At least, I thought I would have been—clearly those jealousies were going to chase me into my marriage.'

'Do you still love him?'

'Angus?' She wrinkled her nose. 'The more time that passes, the more I think I didn't ever really love him. Not as anything more than a friend. But he was the first person in a long time to tell me he loved me.' Her lips twisted painfully. 'He was the first person who made me feel wanted—needed. And I loved that feeling.'

'I have something for you.'

Hannah stifled a yawn, the whirlwind, one-night trip to Paris having been both spectacular and exhausting. She placed her book down on her lap, lifting her gaze to Leonidas's face and feeling that now familiar rolling in her stomach as her nerves exploded. Desire lurched inside her, but it was more than just a physical need.

She longed for him in every way.

'Oh, yeah?'

'Yes.' He crossed the floor of the private jet, propping his hip against the broad armchair opposite her. 'Here.' He reached into the pocket of his shirt and pulled out a small black velvet pouch.

'What is it?' She took it without looking away from his face.

'Open it.'

She did just that, sliding the tip of her finger into the pouch's opening and reaching for the contents. It was tiny and sharp. She tipped it into her palm and smiled. Because there in her hand was the most delicate and beautiful replica of the Eiffel Tower she'd ever seen. A closer inspection showed it was made of diamonds and it was attached to a delicate chain.

'It's truly beautiful,' she said, her voice cracking with emotion.

'I thought you should always have something that brings you so much happiness right by your heart.'

Her heart! Oh, how it flipped and flopped at his thoughtful, kind words.

She felt as though she were soaring high into the heavens, right alongside the clouds outside the porthole windows of this designer jet.

She looked up at him, a smile on her face, holding the necklace out. 'Would you mind?'

He took it from her, arranging it around her neck and clipping it into place. It was a mid-length chain so the stunning charm dangled perfectly between her breasts.

'I love it,' she said sincerely, looking up at him. 'Thank you.'

His smile was the most beautiful thing she'd ever seen. Her pulse fired inside her, but then, his smile flattened and his face assumed a serious, distracted expression. 'You were right on the beach.'

She frowned, searching her memory.

'You said we could make something of this marriage and you were right.'

Her stomach clenched and her heart trembled.

'When Amy and Brax died, my heart died with them, and it's gone—for good. I cannot offer you what I think you deserve, but I can give you enough, I think, for you to want this. For you to be happy.' He crouched down at her feet, clutching her hands, staring into her eyes. 'Look at the life you can lead by my side. Look at how we can raise our child.' He lifted one of his hands to cup her cheek. 'There is enough here to build on, just like you said. We just have to be brave enough to try.'

She felt the once foreign but now familiar sting of tears in the back of her throat. He was speaking softly, as though he were offering a great gift, but all his words did was open up a hole in her heart and make her feel as though she were falling into it completely.

There was something so final and so *limiting* about what he was saying, and the timing of it filled her with despair. Their trip to Paris had been so full of magic and she'd felt so wanted and cosseted, but it had all been a sales pitch, him showing her what he could *give* her to make this marriage appealing. Because he wanted her to be safe, he didn't want the guilt of any harm befalling her, and because he wanted their child close. She'd seen the way he talked about Brax, the genuine love that had filled him—he'd be a great father to their daughter.

This trip hadn't really been about her—he hadn't brought her to Paris because he'd wanted her to see it, he'd done it because he'd wanted her to know what she could expect, being married to him. He'd thought showing her the enormous silver lining of being Mrs Leonidas Stathakis would compensate for the fact his heart 'had died' with his first wife and son.

She bit down on her lip, turning her face away from him without responding, not able to find any words that would express the enormous doubts that were harpooning her soul.

CHAPTER TWELVE

HANNAH HAD BUTTERFLIES in her tummy and they wouldn't quit. She looked at the dress the couturier had brought earlier that day—it was the perfect wedding dress for this perfectly fake wedding.

'Keep it simple,' she had instructed, feeling as if the wedding was enough of a farce without a frou-frou white cupcake dress. And simple it was. A silk slip with spaghetti straps and cut on the bias so it emphasised the curves of her breasts, hips and the roundedness of her stomach. It was not a dress one would wear to a public wedding, in front of hundreds of people.

It was a dress to be worn for a lover. Beautiful, but so incredibly sensual. She ran her fingers over the silky fabric, and then dropped her gaze to the floor, where a pair of rose-gold sandals had been teamed with it. They were casual and comfortable and the perfect bit of whimsy to offset such a stunning piece.

She heard a noise and startled, quickly putting the simple gown back in the wardrobe and slamming the door, spinning around almost guiltily as Leonidas entered their bedroom. When had she started to think of it as theirs, rather than just his? It had been just under a week since she'd arrived on the island and she barely recognised the woman she'd been then.

'Marina has set dinner up on the terrace,' he said. He looked at her as he had on the plane, with a smile that was at ease, as though he'd made his peace with how this would work—he'd slotted her into a space in his mind and he was content with that.

She wasn't his wife by choice, but they could still 'make this work'.

Hadn't she said something along those lines to him, right at the beginning of all this? She'd been happy to take a pragmatic approach then. But something had changed and now the limitations of that sat strangely in her chest.

'Okay.' Hannah returned his smile, but it didn't light up her face as usual.

They walked in silence to the terrace, and when they reached it, Leonidas held a chair out for her.

Mrs Chrisohoidis had gone to a lot of trouble.

Candles flickered everywhere, and fresh flowers had been picked from around the island, filling the terrace with an even more delightful, heady fragrance than usual.

She breathed it in and told herself to relax.

She told herself nothing had changed. They

were two people who were forging a relationship, who were getting married the very next day, and all the reasons for agreeing to this marriage were still there. Aside from the possible danger to her and their daughter, Hannah's desire to provide their child with a father was as strong as ever. To know that if anything ever happened to her, Leonidas would be there—that she would know and love him.

She was doing the right thing—these doubts would lessen once they were married and she could get on with building their marriage.

They would have a lifetime together. A lifetime to make sense of this madness.

But as Leonidas took the seat opposite Hannah, she realised with a terrifying bolt of comprehension that she didn't need a lifetime to make sense of this. He took the seat opposite her and she breathed out, relaxing.

Because he was there; he was near her.

She clutched the stem of her wine glass—filled with ice-cold apple juice—and stared at her groom, as a thousand memories exploded inside her.

Perhaps it was the starlit sky overhead, just like the night they met, but suddenly, Hannah seemed to be looking through binoculars, seeing everything larger and bigger and more true to life.

Why had she slept with him that night?

She'd never done anything like that, and yet one look from Leonidas had made her want to throw herself at his feet. That couldn't be anything other than desire, could it?

So why had she thought of him every day since? Why had he tormented her thoughts and dreams and filled her chest with a strange palpitation?

What was the underlying reason that had made accepting his proposal easy? Beyond the very sensible reasons of security and support, what had really made her agree to this?

Because marriage meant this.

Time with him. Sitting opposite him. Lying with him. Kissing him. Making love to him.

No, not making love.

It was sex. Just sex.

Except it wasn't.

She swept her eyes shut, remembering every kiss, every touch, the way he laced his fingers through hers and stared into her eyes when she exploded with pleasure.

'Hannah?' He leaned forward, curving a hand over hers, and she startled, piercing him with her ocean-green eyes. 'Are you okay? Is it the baby?'

She shook her head, and tried to smile, but her pulse was frantic and her stomach was lurching.

There was no way on earth she'd done something as stupid as fall in love with the man she'd agreed to marry.

Every step of the way he'd told her he didn't want that. Their marriage wasn't about love. It was convenient. Sensible. And yet a rising tide of panic made breathing difficult because they were due to say their vows in the morning, and Hannah knew hers wouldn't be a lie.

In one week…no. Not one week. This thread had begun to stitch its way into her heart that very first night, on Chrysá Vráchia.

She hadn't understood it then—how could she?

It was only now that she comprehended what she hadn't been able to with Angus. Love wasn't a choice, it wasn't a sensible, practical formula one could apply to the 'right' candidate to ensure a lifetime of happiness.

It didn't work like that.

Love was as organic as breathing and laughing. Love was magic and, somehow, it had placed Hannah and Leonidas on the same island at the same time and the chemistry of their bodies had demanded something of them. It hadn't been about chemistry alone, though, she saw that now. He'd offered a one-night stand—and instead, she'd seen his heart and buried a piece of it in her own.

She gasped again, standing jerkily, moving to the balustrade and staring out at the inky black ocean. If it weren't for the sound of the waves, it would have been impossible to know what was beyond the balcony.

'Hannah? *Christós!* What is it?'

She shook her head, unable to speak, definitely unable to put any of this into words. She had to make sense of it herself first. 'I… It's nothing. I just wanted to look at the view.'

She felt his disbelief. 'There is no view. It's pitch black.'

She turned around to face him, surprised to find Leonidas standing right behind her. 'There are stars,' she said softly. 'Lights in the dark. See?'

Her huge green eyes shifted heavenwards, but Leonidas didn't look upwards. He stared at Hannah, worry communicating itself in every line of his body.

'There is also dinner, on the table,' he teased, the words only slightly strained. 'And I am hungry.'

Hannah nodded, even though she wasn't sure she could stomach any food.

'In a moment.' She gnawed on her lip, the realisation of a moment ago doing funny things to her, making her look at him in a wholly new way.

Was it possible to fall in love with someone so quickly? Was love at first sight something she even believed in? Could she be so impractical after everything she'd been through?

It didn't matter how she queried herself.

Her eyes only had to glance to Leonidas and she felt the pull from his heart to hers. She felt a soaring of something inside her that was new and different and refused to be grounded.

She was suffocating, this knowledge desperate to burst from her, but she held it back, keeping her mouth closed even when the words pressed against her lips.

They would marry the next day, and she would say her vows, knowing they were true and honest, and then she would gently show him how she felt. She would give him time to adjust. To feel his way into this.

She exhaled, the sensible approach filling her with relief.

Calmed, she moved back to the table, taking her seat and eating as much as she could—the butterflies in her tummy left little room for food, though.

'Where are you going?' he asked at the door to his room.

Hannah's smile was soft, and inside, she carried the knowledge that was continuing to unfurl inside her. She loved him. She loved him in an everlasting, for-the-rest-of-her-life kind of way. And tomorrow, they'd marry.

'It's the night before our wedding, Leonidas. Don't you know it's bad luck to spend it together?'

His brows arched heavenwards. 'A superstition?'

'Yep.' She nodded. 'And one I intend on obeying. Go to sleep. I'll see you in the morning.'

He groaned, pulling her closer, his eyes locked onto hers. 'I don't want you to go back there.'

He nodded down the corridor, and her heart turned over in her chest. 'Why not?'

She held her breath.

'Because.'

She laughed. 'That's not an answer.'

A frown pulled between his brows but before he could answer, she disentangled herself from his arms. 'It's one night, and then a lifetime.' Her smile almost reached her eyes. Leonidas stared at her, completely silent.

And Hannah stared back, unable to look away, three words whispering through her, begging to be spoken—a question to be asked.

'Goodnight,' she said instead, simply. And she turned away, walking towards the bedroom she'd slept in when she'd first arrived, opening the door and moving into it for what she believed to be the last time.

* * *

Of course it did rain in the Mediterranean on occasion. Summer storms weren't unheard of. But the rain that lashed the side of the mansion woke Hannah before dawn, the unfamiliar ruckus causing her to frown at first. She pushed her sheet back, moving towards the window and staring out of it, so fascinated by the sight of everything that had become familiar looking so foreign and unrecognisable now. It took her a moment to realise what day it was. The significance of the morning.

And then, to remember.

To remember who she was marrying and what he meant to her.

She gripped the wall behind her for support, turning and pressing her back to it as fear tightened inside her.

'When Amy and Brax died, my heart died with them.'

His words had been hammering away at her chest from the inside out since they'd come back from Paris.

She'd decided, the night before, that she would marry him and let things play out. She'd had a sense of confidence, a sureness, that one day he would feel the same as she did.

But what if he didn't? What if he was right,

and his heart was gone for ever, any kind of love no longer in his power to give?

The rain fell harder and she turned to face it, pressing her forehead against the glass. The rain lashed the other side.

What if he didn't love her, and never would? What if he was no longer capable of love? What if she was about to tie herself to another man who was incapable of giving her what she needed?

Panic flared.

When Angus had proposed, she'd been grateful. She'd been grateful that someone loved her and *wanted* her. That someone was choosing her to be their wife and partner. Since her parents had died, she hadn't felt that, and so she'd agreed to marry him out of gratitude rather than love.

She'd known that, and it hadn't mattered. She'd valued feeling wanted above anything else.

But he hadn't really wanted her. Not enough. He'd betrayed her before they'd even said their vows—he hadn't deserved the trust she'd placed in him.

And Leonidas?

Hannah stepped away from the window, padding back to the bed, sitting down on the end of it and looking at her feet. She'd painted her toenails pale pink the day before, thinking how nice they'd look through the strappy sandals she planned to wear for her wedding.

Leonidas didn't want her. If she hadn't been pregnant, they'd never have seen each other again. The thought made her gasp into the bedroom and she held a hand over her stomach, because that very idea seemed impossible to contemplate.

Hannah could no longer disentangle her life from Leonidas's.

They were like roots from neighbouring trees, intertwined and interconnected, dependent on staying where they were for life.

But what if he didn't—wouldn't—couldn't love her?

She'd decided the night before that she would simply wait. Wait for him to realise what they were, what they shared. But could she really do that?

Hannah pushed up from the bed, knowing in her heart what she'd known even over dinner on the terrace.

She couldn't.

She couldn't do this if he didn't know how she felt. She had to be honest with him. She had to… she had to tell him.

And words she'd bit back the night before refused to be silenced now, so she closed the distance between their rooms quickly and pushed the door inwards without knocking, too distracted to wonder how she might find him, her thoughts churning through her.

He was standing with his back to her when she entered, wearing only a pair of grey boxer shorts, his body momentarily robbing her of the ability to think straight. He held a square piece of plastic paper in his hands and, at the intrusion, moved quickly to place it down on the window-sill behind him.

'Hannah.' He was surprised; then worried as he saw the pinched expression on her features. 'Are you okay?'

'No. Yes.' She shut the door behind her, moving deeper into his room, looking at this man and feeling as though everything and nothing made any kind of sense.

'What is it?' He stood perfectly still, staring at her as though he barely recognised her.

'I…need to talk to you.'

His expression didn't shift. 'Okay.'

She nodded, wringing her hands in front of her body, knowing what she needed to say but not exactly sure how to express it.

'I've done something stupid,' she said, shaking her head.

'What is it?' He was quiet, patient, but there was something lurking just beneath his exterior. A darkness that she felt but couldn't navigate.

She expelled an uneven breath and padded across the carpet of his room until she was right in front of him. He stiffened a little.

'Leonidas, the night we met…' She tapered off into nothing, looking at him with eyes that were huge and awash with emotions.

'Yes?'

'It came out of nowhere. I've never done anything like that in my life but I know that there's no way that wouldn't have happened between us. From the moment we literally bumped into each other, I felt this…magnetic pull to you. I know that sounds…ridiculous. But I looked at you and felt like I couldn't *not* go to your room with you. And, once I was with you, like I couldn't not be with you. I feel like, from the moment we met, there's been something bigger pushing us together.'

He was quiet, but she didn't let that discourage her. She'd expected this. She'd known he wouldn't necessarily welcome this confession.

'And then you disappeared and you were angry and I told myself it was for the best. That I was messed up after Angus and so none of this was making sense and I'd made a mistake with you.'

He didn't say it was a mistake, and she was so glad for that, because it would unstitch a part of her soul in a way she'd never recover from to hear those words now.

'But it wasn't a mistake. I never really believed that.' She shook her head slowly, an unconscious smile on her lips. 'I went to London but a part of me stayed on Chrysá Vráchia with you. A part of me stayed with you from that night, and I took some of you with me. I didn't stop thinking about you, Leonidas.'

He stiffened in front of her and there was wariness in his features, a look of panic that was the antithesis of what she wanted, but she pushed on, knowing she needed to do this.

She couldn't marry him and hope for the best—that was what she'd been planning to do with Angus and it had been stupid. Stupid, and a recipe for disaster.

'I don't know if I would have had the nerve to contact you if I hadn't been pregnant. But I do know I never would have forgotten you. I do know I never would have met anyone who made me feel like you did. I always laughed at the idea of love at first sight, but in one hour, you reached inside me and changed who I was. In one hour, you transformed me and I can't marry you today without telling you that I…that this…isn't just about our baby or security or anything so pragmatic and rational as that. This is me offering all of myself to you, for all our lives.' She reached down and laced her fingers through his, as he'd done so often with her.

He didn't speak, though. Her words filled the room, developing a beat of their own, throbbing with the strength of what she had offered him, and every moment that passed with utter silence was like a tendril wrapping around her throat, constricting her airways, making breathing almost impossible. She stood there, her breath raspy, and she waited.

'Why are you telling me this now?'

It wasn't exactly the answer she'd expected, but it didn't matter. Having said what she'd been thinking, she felt as if a weight had been lifted.

'Because I can't not,' she said simply, and his brow furrowed, his expression dark.

'Hannah.' It was a sigh and a plea. 'Don't do this.'

Hannah stood very still, regulating her breathing, trying to stay calm. Because this was important. This mattered. 'I got engaged to Angus for all the wrong reasons. I thought I loved him, I thought he made sense. But nothing about what I felt for him was love. Love isn't a tepid, calm, considered choice. Love isn't a choice at all. Love is a lightning bolt—'

'*Desire* is a lightning bolt,' he interrupted, shaking his head, his expression tense. He took a step backwards, raking a hand through his hair, staring at her with obvious frustration. His body was a taut line of impatience. 'Desire is what you felt for me that night, and it's what you feel for me still. It's clouding your judgment, and you have no experience to discern the difference between that and love.'

'I'm not an idiot,' she murmured. 'I get that there's desire here, too. I know I feel lust as well as love.' She swallowed, trying to order her thoughts. 'One of those things makes my mouth dry when you walk into the room, and the other makes me feel as though my feet are two inches off the ground when you smile at me.'

He wasn't smiling now.

'I was going to marry Angus, you know, even when I wasn't in with love him. I was going to marry him and hope that everything would just work out. I nearly made that mistake once and I can't do it again.'

Now Leonidas was completely still, his face like thunder. 'What are you saying?'

Hannah didn't know, but the words tripped out of her mouth before she could consider them. 'If you don't love me, Leonidas—not even a little bit—if that lightning bolt struck me and me alone, then we can't do this.' Her eyes filled with tears and she found herself powerless to halt their progress. 'If I didn't love you, maybe it would be different, but feeling like I do and marrying you…it would be hell. Every day would be a torment.'

His nostrils flared as he expelled an angry breath. 'We have discussed this. There is so much in our marriage that would be good, so much you would enjoy.' He forced a smile to his face but his eyes remained intent, disconnected. 'You will see the world, travel to places you cannot imagine, and all in five-star luxury…'

'With an army at my back?' she challenged.

'No matter what happens, the army is something you will have to adjust to.'

She shook her head, pushing that aside for the moment. 'That's not enough.'

'It has to be!' He spoke loudly, the words thick with impatience. 'I have told you all along what I am offering. When you came to me in Capri I was clear, and I have been clear all along.'

'Are you saying you still feel that way? That nothing's changed for you since then?'

He regarded her through half-shuttered eyes, lifting his arms and crossing them over his broad, naked chest for good measure. 'Things have changed,' he conceded, finally.

Hannah relaxed, just a little.

'But I don't love you. I'm not free to love you, Hannah. I made a promise to someone and even though she's dead, it doesn't change that. I have told you this as well, and I cannot fathom why you can't just accept it.'

Misery exploded inside her. Hannah drew in a breath, her eyes firing to his, hurt unmistakable in their green depths. He looked away, his jaw rigid as he unfolded his arms and reached for the piece of plastic paper that was on the window-sill. It was a photo, she saw now, and he'd been looking at it right before she'd entered the room.

He handed it to her, his eyes holding a challenge when they met Hannah's.

She turned her attention to the picture slowly, scanning it and frowning as similarities leaped out at her. For the briefest second, she thought the photo was of her, but it wasn't. Close, though.

The woman in the picture was smiling, her lips painted a similar red to the colour Hannah favoured. Her eyes were wide-set and almond-shaped, like Hannah's, and an almost identical shade of green. Her skin was pale, like Hannah's, though Hannah had tiny freckles on her nose and it didn't look as if this woman had any.

Her hair was loose around her face, falling to beneath her shoulders, and it was the exact same auburn red of Hannah's own hair.

Hannah looked at the picture without comprehending, at first.

'Is this Amy?' she whispered, something in the region of her heart bursting, shattering his internal organs with the force.

'Yes. My wife.'

It was just three words, three tiny words, but they were wielded like a machete. Hannah lifted her face to Leonidas's, her skin completely blanked of colour, so that even in the midst of this conversation, he felt a blade of concern.

'Please sit down.' He gestured to the bed, putting a hand on her elbow, but she wrenched out of it, moving away from him, dropping her gaze to the picture. Her fingertips shook and her eyes were filled with tears, making it difficult to focus properly. But she'd seen enough.

Clarity—a different kind of clarity from what she'd experienced last night—settled about her.

'This is what you saw in me that night on Chrysá Vráchia, isn't it?'

Leonidas was quiet.

'If I didn't look like this—' Hannah lifted the photo in the air a little, at the same time she reached for her hair '—you wouldn't even have noticed me, would you?'

Still, he was silent. What could he say? How could he defend this? The evidence was staring back at her.

'Did you think of her when you slept with me?' Her eyes pierced him, the hurt and accusation in them like a physical weapon.

'No.' The word came out gravelled, and it was as if he were being roused from a long way away. 'You are similar, at first glance, but believe me, Hannah, I saw only you.'

She wanted to believe him, but pain was slashing her from all angles.

'But she was in my mind that night. She was a heaviness inside me.' He expelled a long, slow breath. 'That island is where I met her. On New Year's Eve, and it's where I proposed to her. I go there every New Year because I'm a sadist and it's my particular brand of torture. And this year, you walked in and for a moment, I felt like I'd slipped back in time…'

A sob filled Hannah's chest. She was such an idiot! She'd been falling in love with this man, and he'd been living with a ghost.

She groaned, spinning away from him blindly.

He moved after her, gripping her arm, holding her gently, turning her around to face him. 'But that's not why I slept with you.'

His eyes held hers. Even when she wanted to blink away, she couldn't. She was transfixed. Talk about sadism.

'No?' The word was just a whisper. She cleared her throat. 'So why did you?'

'I wanted *you*, Hannah. I've wanted you since that night. I've been tormented by how much I wanted you. And I've hated myself for that. When Amy was killed, I was furious. I swore I would never forget her, never move on with my life. I resisted any woman, any connection with anyone, until you. Even wanting you physically is a betrayal of what I promised myself, of what I owe Amy.'

His words were dragged from him.

'I had a family, Hannah, and they were murdered because of me. Do you think I have any right to close that book and pick up a new one? To simply move on because you're here and pregnant with my child?'

Hannah's heart broke a little more, but for Leonidas this time. He was trapped by his grief, and she couldn't fight that for him. He alone could forgive himself, could work out how to love Hannah and their daughter while still holding Amy and Brax in his heart.

Hannah looked down at the photograph of Amy, and felt a sense of kindredness with this woman, this poor woman. They had both loved the same man, and it bonded them in some way. Hannah handed the photo to Leonidas with an expression that was pure sympathy.

'What would she want?'

He shook his head slowly. 'Amy would want me to be happy.'

Hannah's heart chirruped a little. She stepped forward, so their legs brushed, and she lifted her hands to his chest. 'Then be happy, Leonidas. You'll never stop loving Amy and Brax, and I don't want you to. They're a part of you, and I want them to be a part of our lives. I want to hear more about the little boy who made you laugh, I want to hear about him, I want you to keep him alive within me and one day his sister. You can't live in stasis for ever. I'm here, and I love you, and I'm asking you to open yourself up to this. To look inside your heart and see that I'm there, too.'

She dropped her hands to his, finding his wrists and lifting his palms to her belly. 'I'm asking you to marry me today because you love me, not because you're worried I'll be hurt, not because I'm pregnant. Marry me because you don't want to live your life without me in it.'

He stared at her as though he were drowning, but she was too far away to help him.

He stared at her as though nothing and no one could ever help him. As though he didn't want to be saved.

'I didn't suggest this because I wanted it,' he said, finally, his voice hoarse. 'I can't bear to be the reason someone else is in danger. I shouldn't have slept with you and I shouldn't have got you pregnant, but now that I have and you are, the least I can do is make sure you're safe and looked after.'

His words, so reasonable, so decent, were the polar opposite of what she wanted to hear.

Hannah stared at him for several moments, as the small seed of hope she'd let grow in her chest began to wilt.

'I don't want to be safe and looked after,' she

said quietly. 'At least, that's not a reason to marry someone.'

His eyes narrowed. 'You don't think?'

'No.' She tilted her chin defiantly, even when she'd begun to shake. 'I can take care of myself, and our baby.'

'You have no idea what's out there.'

'And nor do you,' she interrupted forcefully. 'Neither of us has a crystal ball, but I know this: if I stay here and marry you, I'm going to regret it. I'm going to be miserable, and our child's going to be miserable. After my parents died, I went to live with my aunt and uncle and saw for myself how damaging this kind of relationship can be. I won't put our child through that.'

'Damn it, Hannah. You agreed to this…'

'Yeah,' she choked out the agreement. 'But that might as well have been a lifetime ago.'

'Not for me.'

She grimaced. 'No, not for you. And that's the problem. You can do this—you can marry me and sleep with me and hold me through the night and not feel a damned thing.' Tears burned her lashes but she dashed them away angrily. 'I'm not like that. This is real to me.'

'So stay for that. Stay because you love me. I'm not going to hurt you. Stay because you love me and I'll spend the rest of my life taking care of you, making sure you are happy in every way.

Stay here, marry me. I promise you, Hannah, you will have everything you could ever want in life.'

'I'll have *nothing* I want,' she contradicted, but it was sad now, not angry. She blinked, as if she were waking up from a nightmare. 'I can't do this.'

His eyes didn't waver from hers. He stared at her, and she felt a pull within him, a tug between two separate parts of him, and then he straightened, his expression shifting to one of calm control.

'You must.' He hesitated; she felt that pull once more, as if he were at war with himself. 'I cannot allow you to walk away.'

'Are you going to keep me here as your prisoner?'

He stared at her for several seconds. 'No.' His hesitation wasn't convincing. 'But I will fight you for our child. I need to know she's safe, Hannah, and only here, under my protection, will I believe that to be the case. I will sue for custody if I have to. I will do everything within my power to bring her to this island—I would prefer it if you were a part of that. For our daughter's sake.'

She drew in a breath, her eyes lifting to his as those words sliced through her. Words that made her body feel completely weak. The idea of someone as wealthy and powerful as Leoni-

das Stathakis suing her filled Hannah with a re-
pugnant ache.

But then, she was shaking her head, and her
heart thudded back to life.

'No, you won't. You're not going to drag me
through the courts and make my life a living hell.
You're not going to do anything that will garner
the attention of the press, that will expose our
daughter to harm. I don't mean physical harm. I
mean the kind of harm that will befall her when
she's twelve and goes on to the Internet and sees
those stories. Do you think I don't know anything
about the man I've fallen in love with?'

His jaw throbbed.

'You're not going to do that. You're not going
to threaten me and you're not going to take her
from me.' She swept her eyes shut, exhaling as
she realised how right she was. 'You're a good
person, Leonidas, and you're not capable of behaving like that. Whatever you might feel, you
know our daughter belongs with me.'

'And not with me?' he prompted.

'Yes, with you, too,' she said simply. 'And we'll
work that out. We'll work out a way to share her
properly, to give her everything *she* deserves.
For my daughter I would do almost anything—
on Capri, I thought I'd even marry you for her.
I thought needing her to have a "proper family"
and to know her safety to be assured meant this

marriage was essential.' She stared up at him, her eyes suspiciously moist, her voice unsteady. 'But I've got to know myself this week. I finally understand who I am and what I want—marrying a man who doesn't, and says he will never, love me would be a monumental mistake; one I have no intention of making.'

Only ten minutes earlier she'd been readying herself to tell him she loved him, and now Hannah was laying the groundwork for her departure.

'You told me this place is impossible to leave without your say-so. I'm asking you to let me go now. Today. This morning. To organise your plane or your helicopter or your yacht, something to take me away.'

His eyes narrowed; he regarded her sceptically for a moment, and when he spoke there was a bitterness in his words. 'And where will you go, Hannah? To Australia? To your horrible aunt and cousin? Or to London where you know barely anyone?'

Her chest pricked with blades of hurt. 'So you think I should stay here because there's nowhere better to be?'

'I think you should stay here because you want to and because it's best for everyone.'

'Not for me. I won't stay and be an instrument of your self-flagellation, another weapon for your sadism. You punished yourself every year by going to Chrysá Vráchia, and now you plan to punish yourself by having a wife you desire but won't ever love, because it would betray Amy. No, thanks. That's not for me.'

He let out a curse and crossed the room, but Hannah was done. She lifted a hand, stalling him.

'I'm sorry I couldn't disconnect my feelings as well as you did yours. I'm sorry I agreed to this only to change my mind, but I didn't have all the facts.' She reached for the enormous diamond engagement ring that had never really suited her anyway and dislodged it, sliding it over her knuckle and off her hand.

'I'll go back to London,' she said, thinking quickly. 'That makes sense for now. It's close enough that you can see her often.'

He made a noise of frustration. 'I don't want you to go.'

'I know that,' she whispered. 'But can you give me any reason that's good enough to stay?'

He didn't say anything, his eyes running over her face as if he could see inside her soul and find some way to induce her to remain. But there was none—not that he could give her.

'I have a house in London,' he said, his eyes dropping to her lips before he tore them away, looking over her shoulder. 'You should take it.'

'No, thanks.'

'Hannah,' he groaned. 'You're the mother of our child. I need you to be somewhere safe. Somewhere decent. Just…take the damned house for now. We'll sort out the paperwork later.'

'Once she's born,' Hannah compromised quietly. 'But my room is still available. All my stuff is still in it, in fact. I can go back and it'll be like nothing ever happened.' Her smile hurt, stretching across her face, filling her with grief.

'And what of your safety? Do you no longer care for that?'

She felt her stomach twist because he was doing everything he could to get her to stay— but for all the wrong reasons. 'I presume you fully intend to send guards to watch over me?'

He dipped his head in silent concession.

'I will cooperate with you on security, Leonidas.' Her eyes scanned his face. 'I'm not an idiot. If there's even a chance anything will happen to her because of who you are then I want all the help in the world to keep her safe. But that doesn't require marriage. It doesn't mean I have to stay here—with you.' She swallowed, a surreal sense of disbelief that this was happening taking over her.

He swore in Greek, bringing his body to hers, pressing their foreheads together, his eyes shut. 'We can make this work.'

But Hannah knew it was a lie. Not an intentional deceit, so much as a desire to give her what she needed without losing any part of himself. He didn't want to hurt her. He was a good person, and this hadn't been in his plan.

She swallowed past the lump in her throat, a throat that was raw and stinging. 'No, we can't.' She lifted up on her tiptoes then, because she couldn't resist, and pressed a kiss to his cheek. 'But at least we can say we tried.'

CHAPTER THIRTEEN

THERE WERE NO photos of Amy and Brax in any of his homes for one very simple reason. Leonidas needed no photo in order to see them. They were burned into his retinas, his brain, his heart and soul. He saw them readily, and without any effort.

And now, Hannah was there too, and she was imprinted in a way that was impossible to scrub. He fell asleep with her smiling behind his eyelids and woke up with a start, seeing her visceral, deep pain on that last morning.

Her words were a whisper in his ears all day long. *'I'm here, and I love you.'*

Leonidas had become used to the torment of this—and it was a different torment, because, unlike Amy and Brax, Hannah was out there, within reach, a living, breathing person who loved him.

And he wanted her.

He needed her.

But he wasn't messed up enough to know he didn't deserve her. That he couldn't do that to her. Not when she'd fallen in love with him.

She deserved love. Hadn't he known that all along? Hadn't he wished she hadn't fallen pregnant to him purely because he knew she deserved to meet someone who would dedicate their life to loving her? Completely, unreservedly, in every way? She'd find that person, he was sure of it.

And what would happen then? Leonidas wondered. In fact, in the month since Hannah had left the island, Leonidas had thought about that a lot. When he wasn't drinking Scotch and glowering at the ocean, or snapping at the domestic staff and firing off ill-thought-out emails, he was imagining what Hannah's life post-Leonidas might look like.

Twice she'd agreed to marry the wrong man. Twice she'd let her kind, good heart lead her down the garden path.

Would third time be the charm for her? She was mesmerisingly beautiful, kind, funny, intelligent. She deserved someone who loved her. And their daughter?

Pain gripped his chest, because of course their daughter would be a part of that package. If Hannah met and married someone else, his daughter would have a stepfather. The idea filled him with sawdust, but even that wasn't enough. He couldn't go after her simply because he didn't want anyone else to have her.

He wasn't a spoiled three-year-old.

She'd fallen in love with him even though he didn't deserve that love, even though he could never give it back. She'd fallen in love with him and the kindest, fairest thing Leonidas could do for Hannah was accept her decision to leave.

He had to let her go.

'*Christós*, don't go easy on him, will you?' Thanos asked Leonidas.

Leonidas, sitting at the head of the table in one of the boardrooms of their London offices, threw his brother a quizzical expression.

'Did you see his hands shaking? He turned violet from rage.'

Leonidas shrugged. 'He wants to do business with us? Then he needs to lower his rate.'

Thanos laughed. 'I've never seen you quite like this.'

Leonidas compressed his lips. His personal life was a mess but that didn't mean his business life had to be. He'd become some kind of monster since Hannah had left the island—working eighteen-hour days seemed like the best way to put her out of his mind.

Every morning he'd woken to the security briefings, reporting on her whereabouts. Their only communication had been through his lawyers—him transferring a town house in London to her name, her not wishing to accept. He'd wanted to text her. To call her.

Hell, he'd wanted to see her. He'd wanted to see her so badly he'd felt as if he were running a marathon uphill, every single day that passed in which he didn't give into his impulses and get on a flight and go to London, knock on her door and demand she marry him after all.

He was a tyrannical CEO, so why not make it impossible for her to refuse marriage? Threaten harder, demand more.

But every time he imagined doing exactly that, he saw her as she'd been that last morning, her heartbreak evident in every line on her face, her softly spoken words when she'd told him he was a good person, that he would never hurt her.

And she was right about that—he couldn't hurt her. So he'd let her go, as he'd known he should. And every month that passed had filled him with an increasing ache, a desperation that was tearing him apart.

He needed her, but it was a selfish need, just as it had been all along.

He'd taken what he wanted from her, using Hannah to fill in the gaps of his soul without realising he was only adding to her own pains. He was becoming yet another thing she would need to get over.

He wanted to speak to her, but how could he? He took his cues from her and she was refusing to so much as acknowledge his gifts.

This week, however, had been by far the hardest. Three months after she'd left the island, a whole season later, he'd come to London. And he'd gone to bed every night looking out on this ancient city, knowing that she was only miles away. Imagining her, and the roundedness of her belly, the sweetness of her face in repose, the sound of her husky breathing.

He had tormented himself with her nearness— and the knowledge he had no right to see her. That he was here in London and not at her side.

'Leonidas.' He looked up as his brother's assistant entered the room. Belinda, somewhere in her fifties with pale hair and a permanently disapproving scowl, had worked for Thanos for almost a decade and it showed. She was tired and almost on the brink of a nervous breakdown— keeping Thanos's life on the rails could not be an easy occupation. At least they compensated her well for such a chore. 'Greg Hassan's on the phone for you.' She nodded sternly towards the receiver on a bench in the corner of the room.

'Thank you.'

Leonidas moved quickly across the room, telling himself not to panic even as the taste of adrenalin filled his mouth.

'What is it?' He had no time for pleasantries.

'Hannah's been rushed to hospital. Her waters broke.'

'What hospital?'

Hassan gave the name. Leonidas slammed the

phone down and grabbed his coat without saying a word.

'Leo?' Thanos was right behind him. 'What's up?'

'The baby's coming.'

Thanos's smile was huge but Leonidas shook his head. 'It's too early. There's still a month to go.'

Panic wrapped around him. 'Stay here. I'll let you know.'

'Screw that.' Thanos's voice was firm. 'No way.'

Leonidas didn't want company, but he knew better than to argue with Thanos. Besides, he didn't have the energy and he didn't much care. He just needed to get to Hannah, to know everything was okay.

It was peak hour and the hospital was across London. 'Helicopter,' he muttered, shouldering out of the office with an impatience that was overtaking his soul.

Thanos didn't say a thing, simply nodded and took out his phone, giving orders for the helicopter to be readied. On the roof, they climbed into the sleek black chopper and it fired to life.

'Which hospital?' their pilot asked.

Leonidas repeated the name and the pilot lifted off. Thanos turned to Leonidas, his own features taut. 'Try not to worry, Leo. You'll be there soon.'

It didn't feel like soon enough to Leonidas.

Despite the fact the helicopter cut through the sky like butter, he couldn't believe he'd ever let her leave him, leave the island. He couldn't believe she'd gone into labour on her own—that he hadn't been there to help her.

Finally, the chopper touched down on a neighbouring roof to the hospital. The engine wasn't even cut before Leonidas was jumping down, keeping bent low as he ran across the roof.

Thanos caught up to him as the elevator doors opened and neither spoke as the lift careened to the floor. Thanos ran the rest of the way, his heart pounding with every step he took.

'Hannah May,' he said as he arrived, the reception desk mercifully quiet.

'What ward?'

'I don't know.' Leonidas raked a hand through his hair.

'Obstetrics.' Thanos, right behind him, spoke more calmly.

'Let me see.' The nurse moved slowly, pressing her finger to a clipboard, a frown on her face. 'I don't see her.'

'She was brought in earlier. She must be here,' Leonidas demanded.

'Could you check again?' Thanos suggested, putting a hand on Leonidas's chest and pushing him a little away from the counter. His eyes held a warning—a suggestion: *I'll handle this.*

Leonidas paced from one side of the reception to the other, cursing in his head, adrenalin coursing through his veins.

'This way,' Thanos interrupted him, nodding towards the lifts. They went as fast as they could but everything in this old building was slow. When they reached the obstetrics ward and found the corridor they needed to walk down was closed because of mopping, Leonidas almost shouted the hospital down.

'Calm down,' Thanos insisted.

Yeah, right. When they arrived at the desk for the obstetrics ward, Thanos joined the back of a long queue to find out where Hannah was but Leonidas moved through the doors, and he stood stock-still. Because he heard her. He heard her cries and his heart jerked out of his chest.

A scream, pain; he was running down the corridor towards her voice, so close, his hand reaching for the door.

'You can't go in there, sir.' A man was running behind him, an older man, frail. Despite his security guard uniform, Leonidas didn't think he'd have much chance of stopping a terrified six-and-a-half-foot man in the prime of physical fitness.

'Try and stop me.'

'Sir, stop.' A woman now—a nurse. 'This corridor is off limits to visitors.'

'I'm not a damned visitor. My…' *Christós*, what

could he call her? Not his wife. Not his fiancée. She was nothing to him now, just as she'd wanted. His chest rolled. 'My daughter is being born in here.' He hiked his thumb towards the door.

Thanos appeared behind the frail security guard.

'And if you wait in the reception, we'll let you know as soon as your baby arrives.'

He swore angrily. 'No. I want to be in there. Hannah needs me.'

For a moment, the nurse's face flashed with sympathy, but then she was all business again. 'Miss May was very clear on this point. There was no one she wanted called, no one she wanted notified. She told me she is alone.'

Leonidas couldn't meet his brother's eyes. Pain and raw disbelief filled him as he digested this, feeling the rejection of that statement, the line she'd drawn in the sand excluding him from this moment—knowing he deserved no better.

'Tell her I'm here. Please.' The words were hoarse, his stomach rolling, his expression full of desperation.

The nurse relented. 'I will. Please go and wait in reception for now.'

'But I—'

'This is not your call,' the nurse insisted with a quiet firmness in her voice. 'If she wants to do this on her own, you have to accept it.'

Leonidas stared at the nurse, then at the doors, then back at the nurse. Hannah's scream tore through the air and Leonidas felt an agonising need to go to her, to hold her, to do *something*… *anything* to help her.

'Please.'

'It's not my call.' She lifted a hand to his chest. 'I'll tell her you're here. Go and wait for me out there.'

Every bone in his body railed against this; every fibre of his being demanded he stay, that he fight her, that he fight to be with Hannah. But she didn't want him. She was doing exactly what she'd said she would—making her own life.

Despair swallowed him up. He stalked out of the corridor and into the reception room, which was full of happy, waiting family members. Leonidas was the only one who looked as if he could murder someone with his bare hands.

Thanos sat on one of the chairs, his calmness infuriating to Leonidas.

Leonidas was not calm.

Every time he heard her cry out his body was a tangle of pain, of outrage and impotence. How could he let her go through this—without him?

What could he do to help?

Nothing.

But that didn't change the fact that he was living a moment of sheer terror, that he'd spent the last three months in a state of agony and now it had come to this. Her pain filled him and worry—irrational, desperate anger at his own stupidity—drove through him like a blade.

He'd wasted time. He'd gambled. And now he could lose everything.

When a team of two nurses ran through the waiting room and disappeared into the corridor, he followed. When they pushed into Hannah's room, his heart dropped. A doctor followed.

Leonidas couldn't bear it.

He pushed into the room, and almost wished he hadn't when he saw the pain on Hannah's face, the look of sheer terror.

'Sir, I told you, you can't be here.' The nurse who was at Hannah's legs shot him a fierce look but Leonidas ignored her.

He strode to Hannah's side and took her hand in his, his eyes burning into Hannah's.

'I belong here.'

She looked up at him, her expression showing him only pain, only hurt, and he swallowed, fear tearing through him. 'I belong here.'

She didn't say anything, so he stayed; he kept her hand in his and she squeezed it so hard he wondered if circulation might completely stop, half hoping it would so he could feel something like the pain she was enduring.

He stroked her hair at times, and she said nothing to him—nothing to anyone—there were only the indiscernible, guttural sounds of her cries.

She dug her nails into his flesh and gave one last, agonising cry, the nurse lifting a pink and red baby with a shock of dark hair into the air, wiping her quickly with a towel and hitting her on the back until a robust cry emerged into the room.

Tears filled Leonidas's eyes, emotions swirling through him. He looked down at Hannah and she was sobbing, but a smile was on her lips as she held her hands out for their daughter, pulling her to her chest. Leonidas had never seen anything more beautiful, more perfect.

They were his family—they were his.

'You didn't have to come.' Hannah had recovered enough from the delivery to be trying to make sense of what Leonidas was doing at the hospital—and how he'd got there so quickly. Seeing Leonidas again was going to take a lot more recovery time. It had been three months. Twelve weeks. So many nights wondering if she'd done completely the wrong thing, wanting to crumble and beg him to take her back, needing him on every level, loving him enough to take whatever crumbs he would give her.

And in this moment, when her hormones were rioting and she was looking at their beautiful daughter, it took all her wherewithal to remember why she'd left him.

To remember that he didn't love her, didn't want her, that his heart belonged to someone else and always would.

He'd mercifully left the room again after the delivery under threat of the police being called, so Hannah could be cleaned up in privacy and transferred to a different room—one that was smaller and less medical in its design.

She was exhausted, but her heart was bursting—their daughter was asleep in a tiny crib across the room.

'Did you think I wouldn't?'

She shook her head.

'Did you really want to keep me from this?'

She swallowed, looking at him and seeing him almost for the first time. He was so handsome but there was a torment in his face that robbed her of breath.

'I was going to let you know once she was born.'

That her statement had hurt him was obvious, but when he spoke it was quietly, gently, and that somehow hurt even more.

'No doubt.'

He paced across the room and Hannah's eyes followed him hungrily before she realised what she was doing and looked away. A nurse had brought a tea in a few moments earlier, before Leonidas had returned. Hannah reached for it now, cupping the mug in her hands gratefully.

'You were in so much pain,' he said slowly, turning to face her, his eyes roaming over her in the same hungry way she'd been looking at him a moment earlier. 'I thought you were dying.'

'So did I, believe me,' she quipped, but without humour. She sipped her tea then held it in her lap.

Leonidas moved to the crib, staring down at their daughter, and Hannah had to look away— so powerful was the image of the father of her daughter, the man she loved, the pride on his face, the love she saw there...it tore her apart.

Tears filled her eyes and she blinked, sipping her tea again, jerking her head away so she was looking at a shining white wall.

'Three months.' He said the words as though they were being dragged from deep within him. 'You've been gone for three months.'

The tone of his voice had her pulling her face back to him, and she saw pain there, disbelief. Hurt.

'Three months and it has felt like a decade.' He swallowed, his Adam's apple jerking in his throat.

Her own grief was washing over her. 'I had to leave.'

His eyes narrowed. 'Because you love me.'

She swept her eyes shut. 'Yes.' There was no

sense denying it. True love didn't disappear on a whim. It was love. Simple, desperate, all-consuming love.

'*Theos*, Hannah.' He moved towards the bed and she stiffened, bracing for his nearness. She'd come on in leaps and bounds, was learning how to live without him, but she wasn't ready to be touched by him. She couldn't.

'You don't have to be here,' she said urgently, arresting his progress across the room. 'You really don't.'

'I want to be,' he said simply, walking once more. He stood at her side, staring down at her, and her heart flipped in her chest, heavy with love, pain, rejection, fear, need.

'No,' she whispered. 'You don't understand. You can't be here. It's too hard. I don't want you here.'

'Hannah,' he sighed, looking at her, perhaps innately understanding she couldn't bear to be touched by him, not now, not after how he'd rejected her love. 'I've spent the last three months telling myself I was doing the right thing. I knew you were safe, I made sure of that, and I told myself I had to give you what you wanted. I had to let you live your life away from me because I couldn't return your love.'

Hannah made a small, strangled noise of panic.

'And then Greg Hassan called and told me you

were on your way to the hospital and—*Theos, agape mou*—I have never felt anything like this fear and panic.'

He pressed his hand to his chest, staring down at her. 'I was so terrified that something had happened to you and all I could think was how I'd wasted all this time. *Christós*, Hannah.' He dropped his head forward for a moment, catching his breath.

'I've been so focussed on what I lost, so angry at what happened to Amy and Brax, at the fact it was my fault, because of who I am, that I didn't stop to realise how lucky I am to have had that time with them. If I could do it all again, knowing how it would end, I would still choose this life.'

His eyes showed such strong emotions then, and her heart cracked. 'I had a son.' His voice was wrenched with grief. 'A beautiful, perfect boy.'

Hannah sobbed; how could she not? And her eyes shifted to their sleeping daughter, her heart twisting inside her.

'I lost them, and it nearly killed me. I spent four years afterwards living some kind of angry half life. Until I met you, and something shifted inside me, something elemental and important, and it terrified me because I thought the only way I could atone for what happened to Amy and Brax was to keep myself walled off from anyone for the rest of my life.'

Another sob escaped Hannah.

'I avoided human contact, I was rude and arrogant, an impossible bastard. And then I saw you…'

His eyes held hers and Hannah was back on Chrysá Vráchia, the power of that moment, of their connection, searing her blood.

'Greg Hassan called and told me you'd been rushed to hospital and I thought something had happened to you, and I realised I've been shutting myself off to what I have no doubt would be an incredible life with the woman I love because I'm afraid of what *might* happen.'

Hannah's eyes flared wide, her expression showing disbelief and confusion.

'That lightning bolt got me too, Hannah. It struck me and I have been trying to pretend it didn't, fighting you this whole way.'

She shook her head but now he bent down so their faces were level, and so close she could feel his warm breath fanning her cheek.

'You are so brave—do you know that? To have been hurt like you were by Angus and still put yourself out on a limb, telling me you've fallen in love with me—'

She shook her head urgently, and, despite the emotions rioting inside her, she was clear on this point, because she'd had months to think it over, to see it as it was. 'Loving you freed me up to realise I felt nothing like love for Angus. How I feel for you is so different.'

'I know.' He leaned forward a little. 'You love me, and you love me even though I have pushed you away, even though I have been stubbornly clinging to a kind of anger that is ruining my life. You love me even when I took your love and refused to acknowledge I returned it. You have loved me when I was so far from being the man you deserved.'

Hannah bit down on her lip, her eyes holding his. 'Love isn't a choice.' She frowned, lifting a hand to his cheek, because the words had come out all wrong. 'And even if it were, I would choose to love you. You deserve happiness, Leonidas. You deserve it.'

'I wanted to give you everything,' he said quietly. 'When you spoke about your aunt and uncle, your cousin, Angus, all the people who had you in their life and didn't appreciate you, I wanted to scream. You should have the world at your feet; I wanted to give it to you. But you don't really want private jets to Paris, do you?'

She shook her head. 'I mean, that's all well and good, but it's not what really matters.'

'No, it's not,' he agreed, dropping his head to hers, pressing his lips lightly to her forehead. 'All that matters is here, in this room, with you and me. Please tell me I haven't permanently ruined things between us.'

She swept her eyes shut, fear shifting inside her because she didn't want to be hurt again; she didn't want to feel pain.

But nor did she want to live a life without Leonidas in it.

'I'm completely in love with you,' he said. 'Madly, utterly, in every way. I was transfixed by you at Chrysá Vráchia but presumed it was just… that. Infatuation. I couldn't stop thinking about you. I don't know when I fell in love with you, but I do know that from the beginning you have been under my skin and a part of my being. I do know that I want to spend every day we have together showing you that you are the meaning to my life.'

She bit down on her lower lip to stop another sob—a happy one—escaping.

'Life is a gift, and I was wasting it. I don't want to do that any more.'

She expelled a shaky breath, inhaling his masculine fragrance, her stomach swooping and dropping, happiness beginning to flow into her body for the first time in a long time.

'That day on the island—our wedding day—'

She turned to face him, waiting silently for him to finish his thought.

'It was hard. Nothing about marrying you quickly, in secret, away from loved ones, felt like what I wanted. Making you my wife, yes. But like that?' He shook his head, and then reached into his pocket, pulling out a black velvet box. Hannah's eyes dropped to it, her smile transforming her face.

'So I would like to ask you again, Hannah, if you would do me the honour of becoming my wife. I love you with every single part of me. My heart and soul are, and always will be, yours.' He took her hand and lifted it to his lips, pressing a kiss to her inner wrist. 'You brought me back to life and made me myself again. But better, because you've taught me so much about compassion and love, respect and patience. You are so much more than I deserve.'

At that, she shook her head silently, because her throat was filled with tears and she wasn't sure she'd be able to get any sensible words out.

'But I will spend the rest of our lives, however long that may be, striving to be good enough for you, *agape mou.*'

Hannah sobbed then, as he handed the ring box to her.

She hadn't loved her engagement ring—it had been so enormous and flashy. But she'd come to love it because it had promised a future with Leonidas. She cracked open the box and smiled, because it wasn't even the same ring.

Instead there was a single diamond, still large

but not break-your-finger huge, surrounded by a circlet of emeralds.

'It's beautiful,' she whispered, her eyes filling with tears.

'Two weeks after you left the island, I was in Athens. I saw it in a window and bought it without even realising what I was doing. I have been carrying it around ever since, as though it made you close to me in some way.' His smile was rueful. 'I told myself I could give it to you as an "I'm sorry" gift, if nothing else. But in my heart, I imagined you wearing it on this finger.' He ran his hand over hers. 'And wearing it as a promise to become my wife, to live this life by my side.'

She sobbed then, and held her hand out, so he could slide the ring onto her finger; it fitted perfectly.

'And this is my promise to you,' he said gently, fixing her with a look that seared her soul. 'I will love you and cherish you, be faithful to you, care for you, protect you, adore you and worship you for as long as we both shall live.'

Hannah nodded, still too choked up to respond with words. And really, what words were needed? They'd said all that was necessary and, more importantly, each felt the truth of their declaration, deep inside their beings—and always would.

The only thing left was to marry, and to live happily ever after.

EPILOGUE

'I KNOW YOU said you wanted me to see the world, but this is more than I ever imagined.'

'Do you like them?'

Hannah gave her husband a droll look before turning back to the golden vista beneath her, her green eyes taking in the flat expanse of the Egyptian desert before focussing on the familiar peaks of the ancient Pyramids. The helicopter hovered at a distance, giving a perfect vantage point over them.

'They're stunning,' she said simply. Because they were. It was hard for Hannah to say which of the countries they'd visited in the past eighteen months was her favourite. They all had a special place in her heart, and for different reasons. Going to a special opera performance at the Coliseum had been incredible, a private tour of the Pantheon had taken her breath away, exploring New York with Leonidas by her side, coming to know his Greek island as though she were a local, snorkelling off the shore, swimming in the pool, learning to speak his language and enjoy his food—it had all been remarkable: but all the more so for having Leonidas by her side.

And though she'd planned to wait to tell him her news, with the ancient Pyramids glistening beneath them, a testament to humanity's strength, intelligence, and determination, Hannah felt the words burst out of her.

'I got an email two days ago.'

'Yes?'

She nodded, pride making her eyes sparkle. 'My application was accepted.'

'Your application…?'

She nodded, excitement a thousand arrows darting beneath her skin. 'Law school.'

Leonidas's smile transformed his face and Hannah's heart clutched at the sight. Love was a lightning bolt, yes, but it was also this—a genuine, complete desire to see your loved one succeed in life. Leonidas had been Hannah's champion, he had supported her, overcome her doubts when she'd worried she wouldn't have what it took to apply for her degree, and then when she'd doubted she'd be able to meet the study schedule.

He'd moved all the pieces effortlessly so she could apply, and still be hands-on with their daughter, Isabella.

Her dreams had become his dreams.

'I never doubted for one second that you would be accepted.'

'Because you're Leonidas Stathakis and I'm your wife?' she teased.

'Because you're *you*,' he corrected, leaning forward and kissing her. 'Brilliant, intelligent, motivated, fiercely strong.'

Hannah's heart was flying higher than the Pyramids, way up in the sky.

She was going to achieve her dreams, and even though she liked to think she could have done this on her own, she was so glad it was happening this way—she was so glad she got to share it all with Leonidas.

Hours later, back on the yacht in the Red Sea, with Isabella fast asleep, Hannah reading in the armchair, Leonidas looked at his wife and felt a quick surge of panic, familiar to him now, whenever he contemplated how close he'd come to losing all this.

He had almost shut the door on love and happiness in life because of fear.

He would never make that mistake again.

* * * * *

If you enjoyed
The Greek's Billion-Dollar Baby
by Clare Connelly
look out for the second instalment in her
Crazy Rich Greek Weddings duet

Bride Behind the Billion-Dollar Veil
Coming soon!

And why not explore these other
Clare Connelly stories?

Bound by the Billionaire's Vows
Bound by Their Christmas Baby
Spaniard's Baby of Revenge
Shock Heir for the King

Available now